SEBASTIAN

CRASH TEST DUMMY

SEBASTIAN

CRASH TEST DUMMY

DAVID PHOEBE

A special thanks to Richard Ellis and Rachael Gregory.

National Library of Australia Cataloguing-in-Publication entry:

> Author: Phoebe, David, author.
> Title: Sebastian : crash test dummy / David Phoebe
> (author).
> ISBN: 9780987374622 (paperback)
> Target Audience: For primary school age.
> Subjects: Crash test dummies--Juvenile fiction.
>   Adventure fiction.
> Dewey Number: A823.4

Cover design by David Phoebe.

This book is dedicated to:

Anyone who has been in a hit and run −
struck down by a car, or by real life.
I don't recommend either.

01

There was no screeching of wheels before impact.

Holding Madison's hand, Astrid crossed with her three-year-old daughter. Astrid's hip broke first, buckling the car bonnet. Her leg snapped against the grill. Madison's body bent against her mothers, her head smashing into a headlight, which imploded. Astrid's body bent, her shoulder crumpling into the hood, followed by her head lashing into the windscreen. Shattered glass entered the cabin as the car skidded out of control. Bursts of smoke came from the rear tyres.

Once the accident was in motion, no one could stop what was happening. No one knew how to stop it. Astrid punctured the windscreen. The top half of her body entered the cabin. The roof sliced her arm off at the elbow, sending it flying to the ground behind the car. Her body collided with the passenger. The sound of the cracking bodies was lost in the noise of impact.

Madison twisted under the front tyre, her small legs wrapping around each other as she rolled. The rear wheel locked in place and dragged her, scraping her face along the hard ground. The car crumpled as it slammed in to a barrier, sending Astrid flying back through the windscreen and into the wall. The car had rippled into a new shape, leaving a mess only skilled experts would be able to untangle as they tried to understand exactly what had happened.

An eerie stillness fell across the scene of the accident as the last scatterings of glass came to rest on the hard ground. Silence.

Astrid didn't look like she should; her body was broken and bent. Lying beside the car, her arm was twisted back under her head. Her right foot was closer to her face than any right foot should be. Only Madison's tiny hand could be seen protruding from near the tail end of the car. Bursts of white strobe lights reflected off the floor, illuminating her pinkish-orange latex skin. Her head jerked forward as her eyes flicked open. Twisting her neck, Astrid turned her face towards the ceiling and crunched her way to her feet.

The crowd erupted with applause. Dummies cheered. Humans cheered. Everyone cheered. This was the moment the dummies had been anticipating. On large screens around the crash test arena everyone watched the crash over and over again. Slow motion. Fast motion. Multiple camera angles. The Crash Test Dummies became more excited with each viewing and applauded louder.

Strobe lights flashed over the crash floor and music

filled the arena. Exhaust fumes and dry ice rose in the air like a ghostly fog. Yellow laser lights lowered over the dummies, weaving patterns across their faces and bodies. Spotlights flared on the crash floor. Dummies crashed into each other as they jostled with excitement, bumping chests and knocking each other off balance.

Astrid back flipped over the car, landing centre stage. Swiping up her left arm from the crash floor with her right hand she waved it to the audience. Madison pulled herself out from under the car, as the dummy driver pulled himself through the busted windscreen. Standing in front of the car, they gave a bow to the audience.

"Welcome to your graduation," Astrid's voice trumpeted.

Astrid pressed her limp hand to her lips and blew kisses to the crowd as the dummies left the crash floor. The crowd of Crash Test Dummies revelled as the lights flickered over them. Floodlights illuminated the crash scene. The yellow and black impact stripes on the side of the car now zigzagged across the red paint. Broken pieces of the vehicle had settled on the concrete and the rearview mirror finally dropped off.

Glass doors opened on the balcony. Backlighting and swirling mist silhouetted a figure as it stepped out onto the platform.

The CEO of CrashCorp Automotive Facility, Lucinda Craven, stood in the centre of the balcony as the spotlights turned and focused on her. She raised both hands. The dummies fell silent.

"Look what we have before us?" Lucinda's voice boomed through a microphone, echoing throughout the arena. Her eyes glanced over the car wreckage lying beneath her. "Carnage. Carnage and a waste of life. We can only analyse what remains and try to gain knowledge from this destruction. From disaster often comes great understanding. It's my beloved Crash Test Dummies who we have to thank for our understanding of the secrets of crashing."

Lucinda allowed the Crash Test Dummies to enjoy their moment. The lights on the crash floor dimmed. The applause died down.

"Why wish for carnage, when we can have something beautiful?" said Lucinda. "Nothing pleases me more than honouring those who have given everything to ensure safety. You've worked tirelessly to protect the lives of millions. You have done what no one else can. For that, you truly deserve our respect."

The dummies cheered. The spotlights focused towards the stage at one end of the crash floor, where several dummies stood, doing their best to contain their pride.

"These dummies stand before you as heroes," said Lucinda. "True heroes. This crew has been exemplary. Normally, only two or three dummies graduate together; ready to take their privileged positions in Elcycer, the *Land of Heroes*. Because of the dedication and the effort of this group, we are proud to grant them all entry into Elcycer.

"These fine Crash Test Dummies are the best of the best. They have displayed their brilliance in the art of crashing.

Tonight, Elcycer belongs to them. Let's hear it for our largest graduating group ever."

Sebastian stood proudly on the stage with his son, Jupiter, and the other graduates. The new heroes absorbed the praise of their workmates, both human and dummy. Once dummies had reached such a great height they were given a victory ceremony, where all the other Crash Test Dummies and factory employees gathered in the crash arena to celebrate their efforts and forever recognise them as heroes. Graduation was a dream come true for any Crash Test Dummy. They would be guaranteed a place in Elcycer, where they would hang out and live a long life amongst all the other heroes who had come before them. In the *Land of Heroes*, they would find themselves surrounded by other such renowned Crash Test Dummies such as: Charlie Crasher, who pioneered many of the crash tests still in use today; Gyro Jim, who flew through the air after a crash and landed with the skill and flair of a professional gymnast; and Mangled Martha, who gave dummies the saintly loving care and repair after a hard days crashing, and also had a passion for testing big rigs.

"Hey Sid," called Sebastian. "Don't worry, buddy. You'll be up here soon."

Sid slunk behind his fellow Crash Test Dummies, hiding from the spectacle of graduation. He knew he would never be a hero and make his way to the gates of Elcycer. He imagined his time at CrashCorp would be endless. He had watched other dummies arrive after him and graduate long before he could ever have a chance to qualify. Tonight his best friend would leave the factory. Sid would possibly be seeing Sebastian for the last time, something that made him a little nervous, along with all the other things that made him nervous.

Sebastian had become a living legend at the factory. He had crashed enough things, like cars and trucks and motorbikes and forklifts into things like walls and poles and other dummies. He had gone through windscreens, hit walls and been run over by trucks. He had clocked the highest number of crashes any dummy at the factory had ever recorded. When it came to crashing into all things, Sebastian was number one.

Lucinda stepped back through the glass doors of the balcony and re-emerged through another set of doors on the crash test floor. The graduating dummies formed a rough line as she greeted them on stage. She walked along and thanked all seven of them individually.

"Sebastian. Thank you for your dedication and loyalty. Your work here will go on to benefit many more to come."

"Thank you, Ms Craven," said Sebastian, basking in the attention.

"You will be well taken care of at Elcycer."

"No one has ever come back to complain about it."

"No, I am sure they haven't. Thank you and take care," Lucinda smiled, as she hung a medal around Sebastian's neck. The medal was a symbol that the dummies no longer desired to become heroes, having now achieved their goal.

Lucinda moved onto the next dummy. Sebastian lifted up Jupiter into his arms and they waved to Astrid and

Madison, who stood on the edge of the crash floor. Madison held her mother's hand, with Astrid's broken elbow resting on the floor. She hugged her mother's good leg.

Once all the dummies shook hands with Lucinda, and the medals had been placed around their necks, the graduating dummies huddled together and a camera flash lit up the room as they were photographed. The dummies left the stage with great pride, marching down a long ramp and out of the crash arena. The sound of the audience quickly faded as the fire doors slammed closed.

"I'll just take these medals for safekeeping," said a guard, collecting them as each Crash Test Dummy passed. "You will get them back when you reach Elcycer."

The dummies marched through the cinder block corridors under CrashCorp and towards the delivery dock. Clumsy footsteps echoed in the long white tunnels. Florescent lights stripped the colour from their blue crash test suits and made their skin look pale. A truck waited in the dock.

"Is this Elcycer?" asked one dummy.

"Not yet," said a workman. "Jump inside. You'll be there in no time."

The dummies climbed into the large cargo hold of the truck. The large back doors slammed closed and a hand pushed down on the lock. An orange warning light flashed as the security door rolled up. The truck drove across the empty car park, through the gates, and turned into the night.

02

Max's shadow stretched along the walls as he walked through the night. The constant hum of the city was punctuated by the sounds of dogs barking and car horns bleating in the distance. A car revving reverberated through the air before disappearing into the background bustle. Clouds moved over the city, lit up by the strings of streetlights criss-crossing the suburbs. Most people were asleep. Some lights still lit up windows. Max wondered what kept these people awake. Why didn't they sleep? Shift work? Infomercials? Homework? Insomnia? Coffee? Worry? Maybe it was a mixture of many or all. Everyone had a reason for being awake at this small hour.

Climbing up a stone covered embankment, Max headed across the train tracks. He followed along the factory walls. Every last accessible section was filled with paintings, pictures, art, murals, tags, stencils, graf or graffiti.

Whatever you want to call it. Vampires bit into crystal skulls. Escher-style paintings linked impossible staircases. Tiny robots smiled out to commuters on the trains. Max could only walk so far before he would have to avoid railway workers, or wander into the gaze of security cameras monitoring the tracks. Cargo trains would radio back to base if they spotted someone walking along the lines. If they didn't send their own people, they would send the police.

Sliding down the embankment, Max entered a dead end street in the industrial estate. It was more than an estate. It stretched out to the edge of the city. Large concrete buildings, designed for functionality rather than looks, crowded around him, creating a shadow land for him to slip between. Bare ground and fencing stretched between each warehouse. At this time of night even the buildings were sleeping.

Max felt the cool breeze glide over his arms, giving him goose bumps. The whole area was empty now; it belonged to him. Normal life had been turned off. The rules of daylight hours no longer applied. For just a few hours the whole world held still.

Max's shadow moved over empty streets and up factory walls. He had been in this area often, riding his bike on weekends, graduating to a skateboard, and now to night walking. He knew his way around and the places to hide. The soles of his shoes on the asphalt echoed between the walls. All things were clearer in the forgotten hours. Colours simpler, sounds sharper, and the air cleaner.

From and intersection on top of a hill Max looked over the city. Traffic lights around him changed automatically, signalling to invisible cars. Cars could come from any direction, their headlights announcing their approach. Floodlights lit up the steel pipes of far off refineries as they pumped out steam. The clouds changed from sulphur yellow in the west to a dull chalky glow as they reached the city skyscrapers, which appeared in front of him like toy towers in the distance.

The spray paint marbles rolled in rhythm with Max's footsteps as he searched through the streets. There was still enough time before the sun rose and the early morning workers began to snake their way through the streets. Max found what he was searching for. A wall. A blank wall everyone seemed to have forgotten about. Max knelt down and unzipped his backpack. He searched for the colour he wanted, shook up the spray can, and pressed firmly on the nozzle.

03

"Tonight you will witness the dawn of a new era at CrashCorp," Lucinda spoke into the headset.

Lights shone out from behind Lucinda as she reappeared on the balcony after sending off the graduating Crash Test Dummies. Fog rolled onto the crash floor. Two silhouetted shapes appeared beside Lucinda. They looked like humans. They looked like Hybrids. They looked like something other. Something new. The fog settled on the crash floor, twirling its way through the spectators' legs. A spotlight turned towards the command deck. Two dummies stood before the audience like brand new statues.

"I would like to introduce you to the new generation of Crash Test Dummies," said Lucinda. "The Thor range. Thors are the greatest advancement of Anthropomorphic Test Devices ever witnessed. These dummies are a significant progression, and will see CrashCorp head in a new direction of unprecedented opportunities."

Several Thor dummies marched onto the crash arena floor and stood in a straight line. Clean sharp moulded bodies stood strong under the bright lights.

"Who are they?" asked a dummy. The Hybrids looked at each other.

"I can see some of you Hybrids are unsure about what is exactly going on," said Lucinda. "We have all worked hard at CrashCorp to understand what occurs during an accident, and how we can prevent them from happening. It's only through your hard work and dedication we've been able to achieve this. Over the next short while, we will be phasing in the Thor range. This will pave the way for future generations to live happy and fulfilling lives. And through this leap forward, all Hybrids will be pleased to know this will hasten your advancement towards reaching Elcycer."

All the Hybrids cheered. After the speeches, the Hybrids welcomed their new dummy friends, before heading back to their sleeping quarters to be put away on their suspension hooks for the night. Tomorrow they would be ready for more crashing and one day closer to reaching Elcycer.

*   *   *

The CrashCorp truck panted along the quiet night streets, heading out through the industrial zone. The dummies could not see out into the world, not that they had ever seen outside of the factory before. They could feel the vibration of the truck as it rumbled beneath them.

"They must be getting ready to crash," said Piston Pete. "I've never gone so far before without crashing."

The seven of them sat in the back, jolting as the truck stopped and started, started and stopped, through the quiet streets.

"I can't wait," said Sebastian. "Time to finally be with the greatest dummies of all."

"Heroes forever," said Jupiter. "I'm going to show all my friends my medal."

"You'll have to wait for them to become heroes and join us," said Sebastian. "It may be a long time."

"Yeah, but I can go back and see them," said Jupiter. "And they can come over and crash with me too."

"Nope, afraid not, son," said Sebastian. "Only heroes enjoy the company of other heroes. It's one of the privileges of being a hero."

"I can't see my friends?"

"Nope."

"Doesn't sound like much of a privilege," said Jupiter, slouching against the truck wall.

"When we reach Elcycer you can crash anytime you like," said Roadkill Rachael. "And you will have plenty of dummies to make friends with."

"Just think about all the amazing crashes waiting for you. That will take your mind off it," said Banged-Up Bob, as he ruffled Jupiter's head. "Here's to eternal crashing."

The dummies gave each other high-fives. Jupiter sat with his arms crossed and ignored the head rubbing and the high-fives coming in his direction.

The truck tipped forward, changing gears as it struggled up a hill. The brakes eased the truck to a stop as it reached a set of traffic lights. The clang of the rear door caused all the dummies to turn in unison. One of the doors had become unsecured and slowly glided open, revealing the night streets.

"Is this Elcycer?" asked Jupiter.

"I'm going to have a peek," said Sebastian. "My first look at the Land of Heroes."

The other Crash Test Dummies smiled at each other as Sebastian slid over to the door, opened it wider and peered out.

"Are you sure we have arrived, Sebastian?" asked Roadkill Rachael.

"Give me a look," Jupiter said, jumping off his seat.

"What's it like?" asked Piston Pete.

"It's full of walls," said Sebastian. "So many walls to crash into."

A cloud of exhaust rumbled into the air, as the truck lurched forward through the green traffic light. Sebastian toppled, landing headfirst on the road. Shuffling to his feet, Sebastian scanned his surroundings. He had never seen anything as enormous as the sky. He had never imagined the world to be so large, finishing all the way beyond the lights at the bottom of the hill.

"Dad, grab my hand," cried Jupiter, as he tried to reach

out.

Running after the truck, Sebastian stumbled forward, his face planting itself firmly on the road. Crash Test Dummies were good at crashing, but coordinating themselves so they can run is something most never mastered. Scrambling back onto his feet he did his best to run after the truck as the other dummies peered out. Almost reaching Jupiter's small hand, Sebastian became tangled up in his own legs and made one last spectacular dive into the asphalt. The red taillights of the truck shrunk to become lost in the city lights expanding out before him.

"Wait," called Sebastian. "You forgot about me. I'm a . . . I'm a . . . hero."

Giant lampposts shone down on Sebastian as he stood in the middle of the intersection. The only sound was the traffic lights clicking over. Sebastian looked around. A screwed up piece of paper scurried along the gutter, pushed by the breeze. Stars floated in the inky sky. And Sebastian realised he was completely and utterly alone.

The night seemed endless and empty. Sebastian grew tired of walking the deserted streets. He didn't feel like a hero anymore, he just felt very small in this large new world. A few trucks passed, sometimes he chased them. He fell over less and less as he became used to the whole running thing. Some of the trucks looked like the one he had fallen from, but he couldn't be exactly sure if any were it. He noticed one kept stopping to collect rubbish bins that lined the road, giving Sebastian time to catch up.

"Hey guys," Sebastian waved.

Two men hanging from the back of the truck stared at Sebastian, as the truck grunted forward a few metres.

"Hold on a sec," Sebastian yelled.

A giant hydraulic fork lowered down the side of the truck. It lifted a green wheelie bin and dumped the contents into the top of the garbage truck.

"Looks like we've got another live one, guys," one of the men said, as the truck shunted forward.

Sebastian was able to keep up with a steady untangled jog.

"I need to find something," Sebastian shouted.

"Once it's in the truck it's gone for good. You gotta be careful about what you chuck out." The garbo (or garbologist or sanitation engineer, if you prefer to use their correct title) signalled for the driver to move on. "Whatever it is you're lookin' for, Bud, it's gone for good."

"I'm not looking for a thing, I'm looking for a place," Sebastian said.

"Do we look like tour guides?" the other garbo shouted.

"Do you know where the Land of Heroes is?"

"The land of what?" One garbo yelled over the sound of squealing brakes.

"The Land of Derelicts is what you might be looking for." Both garbos laughed.

"At least the crazies make the trip a little entertaining," the garbo said to his workmate.

"Where can I find the great land?" asked Sebastian.

"Okay, Jack, this ones full, back to the depot," yelled the garbo as he banged his fist on the side of the truck. He pushed a button starting the trash compactor, compressing the rubbish into the trucks belly. Riding the side of the truck he shook his head as the truck drove away.

04

The spray can hissed as it moved over the wall, slowly transforming the concrete canvas. Max worked from a final diagram he had constructed from several drawings sketched in his black book. He had created the outline, allocating colours that would become mostly hidden by the later layers. He worked with caution, not only to the detail of the design, but also out of fear of being spotted by random headlights that swept through the streets. Max lost track of time when creating. Time didn't matter, only the final result did. His piece took shape. The hollows looked large and over painted, waiting to be filled in. Other sections had yet to give a hint at what they would become.

Max swapped cans and used a fat tip to fade in the colours. He had spent two months designing his piece, hiding out in his bedroom, filling up his book until he had the image he wanted. It was his first piece of graffiti.

Spending nights in the garage, his face covered with a dust mask, Max practiced on an old cupboard door. He cut lines until he had the effect he wanted. He rehearsed by completing a section at a time. Once he knew how to paint each section, he could tighten them up and finish the job in one hit. There was no writing, just images and characters.

Max changed to a skinny tip and began adding detail. Shaking the can, the sound of the marble echoed through the air. Hearing a car approaching, Max jammed the paints into his backpack and ran into a doorway. With his back to the wall, he watched the car glide passed. His heart raced. The lights gleamed over where he hid, barely missing him, before returning him to the shadows. Max listened for a minute until he was sure he was safe. His piece was still a long way off being finished. The sun would soon rise and he still had to make it home to give the appearance he was ready for school. The day would be long and tiredness would seek its revenge, but the night would make it worthwhile.

Max shook the can and readied to press on the cap.

"Is that your wall?" a voice sounded.

Max spun as he jumped back, almost falling against the wet paint. A silhouetted man stood on the roadway. Max raised the spray can in defence.

"Come near me and I'll blind you," Max's voice shook.

The figure took a step closer.

Max pressed the nozzle. Only gas escaped from the empty can. Pulling his arm back, Max threw the can. It hit the target in the face, bounced onto the road and rolled towards the gutter. Max expected at least some kind of reaction, but there wasn't any. Not even a flinch. Then the face came into the moonlight. Not sure whether it was out of fear or wonderment, Max froze.

"What are you?" Max asked.

"I'm a Hybrid-III, fifty percentile male, the finest there is," replied Sebastian. "And a hero!" Sebastian's rubbery face smiled in the moonlight. Max noticed circular crash test symbols on the side of his head.

"A what?" Max said, almost dazed.

"A world class anthropomorphic test device or ATD," Sebastian said. "Generally referred to as a Crash Test Dummy. And you are clearly a miniature human. Do others come as short as you?"

Max noticed Sebastian's name embroidered on his blue overalls.

"Sebastian?" Max said to himself.

"You know me?" Sebastian beamed. "I do have quite the reputation."

The darkness evaporated in a burst of floodlights. Red and blue swirls flashed on the walls. *Whoop.* The siren stole the silence. Unable to see through the glare of the lights, Max was right to assume it was the police.

"Run," yelled Max, heading for an alley. Sebastian ran as best he could. Not realising he was meant to follow Max, he headed in the wrong direction. "This way."

Max grabbed Sebastian's hand, which felt cold and rubbery, and pulled him along. Lights saturated the alley. The police car was too large to make it through the narrow entrance that was also blocked by bollards. The pair turned the corner and fled down the back of the buildings. Sebastian found it hard to coordinate his feet and stumbled along behind Max.

Pushing up the lid of a dumpster, Max looked inside. The dumpster was empty.

"Quick. Get inside," Max ordered. "Hide here until it's safe."

Sebastian fell into the dumpster. Max let the lid drop.

Max ran, turning wherever he could in the maze of alleys and paths hidden by the buildings. Lights ghosted passed him. Hearing the sound of the cans rattling in his backpack, Max yanked it off. With a couple of swings of his arm, he launched the backpack into the air and listened to it land on a factory roof. Darting through the shadows he headed towards the train line, hearing the sound of footsteps behind him. He didn't dare look back.

Max leapt onto a loose cyclone fence that was barely able to hold itself up, only to have it fall back on him. The police helped him the rest of the way to the ground. Caught. Pulling him to his feet, an officer held Max by his collar. Max struggled.

Max felt himself held back by the officer's hand.

"What's your name, son?" the officer gruffed.

Max pursed his lips.

"Look, I'm starting with the easy questions. But, if you want to make this difficult, then that's fine by me. So, again, what is your name?"

"Max Alderson."

"Okay Max," said the female officer, "that wasn't so hard. I'm Constable Grieves and this is my partner Senior Constable Billing. What's your reason for being out here at this time of night?"

Max cast his eyes down to the cobble stone path.

"Where's your friend?" asked Billing.

"I don't know. He's not my friend," Max replied, avoiding eye contact.

"Then who is he?" Billing asked, shining a torch in Max's eyes.

"I don't know," squinted Max. "Just some guy. I think he was in fancy dress or something. He ran off."

Senior Constable Billing hid his frustration, but Max was far from the first teenager he had dealt with.

"Do your parents know where you are at this time of the morning?"

Max didn't say anything. Both officers already knew the answer.

"What are you doing out here?" asked Grieves.

"I was just going for a walk."

"Then why did you run?"

Keeping his eyes on the ground, the officers waited for a response Max wasn't willing to give. Being a fourteen-year-old boy, walking alone in an industrial estate at night, the police were correct in being more than a little suspicious.

"Did you spray paint that wall?" Billing asked.

"Do I look like I have any spray cans on me?" Max felt slightly relieved he had thrown away his backpack.

"Then why do you have a dust mask hanging around

your neck?" asked Grieves.

It was a small detail Max had forgotten about in his panic.

"To stop getting a flu." Even Max knew this excuse was lame, especially as it was the end of summer and the flu season was still a long way off.

"We need to get you into the car and get you home. Then we will see if we can get some sensible answers," said Billing.

Max broke away from the officer's grip and ran. The fence failed again and he found himself back on the ground with help from the police.

"No," yelled Max. "I'm not getting in the car."

"This will be a lot easier if you comply," said Grieves. "I think we'd all like it if you didn't end up in handcuffs."

"You can't make me get in there," said Max.

"Look, son," said Billing, "it's either the patrol car or the divisional van. And if we have to get the van out here, you won't be going home. You'll be going to the watchhouse to be locked up. You understand me? I'm not here to play games."

With some effort, some considerable effort, the officers managed to get Max into the back of the patrol car. With his head on his knees, Max trembled as they drove him home. The tears he tried to force back ran through his fingers as the street lights raced by.

05

On the outskirts of town the CrashCorp truck reached its destination. The engine throttled down as it approached the gates. The driver pushed his foot on the clutch, pressed the brake pedal and brought the vehicle to a stop in front of the guard booth. Pulling on the hand brake, the driver leant out the window and handed the security guard a clipboard.

"Busy night?" said the driver.

"Run off my feet," answered the security guard, stepping into the small umbrella of light, which in the summer darkness attracted disorientated insects.

Taking a pen from his shirt pocket the guard walked to the back of the truck. He noticed a door ajar. Pulling at the latch, he let out a groan underneath his breath. The Hybrids sat in the back of the truck as he called their names.

Roadkill Rachael? *Check.* Busted-Up Bob? *Check.* Impactor? *Check.* Piston Pete? *Check.* Jupiter? *Check.* Crumpler? *Check.*

"Sebastian?"

"Sebastian?"

"Sebastian?" he called again. All Hybrids sat still, ignoring Sebastian's absence.

"I'd personally like to welcome you all to Elcycer. Enjoy your stay." The Hybrids smiled at each other, excited to arrive. The guard slammed the door closed, making certain the latch clicked into place.

"What about dad?" asked Jupiter.

"Don't worry, he'll find his way here," said Roadkill Rachael. "All heroes do."

Stepping back around to the front of the truck the guard looked at the driver and sighed.

"They're not all there," said the guard.

"I know," said the driver. "They're nuts, but you've got to work with what you're given."

"No. They're not all there. One is missing."

Jumping from the truck, the driver's boots crunched on the driveway gravel.

"I don't understand," said the driver. "They were all there when we left."

"It might be because one of the doors was wide open when you pulled in. Just a guess."

Ripping on the latch the driver pulled the door open to see all the Hybrids turn to look at him. Pointing at each of them, he mouthed the numbers as he counted.

" . . . four, five, six." He counted again. "Damn. Where's Sebastian?"

The dummies steered clear of giving him an answer.

"We'll get these guys processed, then I'll call the factory. Hopefully he's been left behind at CrashCorp. For your sake."

Pressing the button to open the gate, the guard let the truck through. The Hybrids had finally made it to the place all Crash Test Dummies dreamed about. They had made it to Elcycer.

*   *   *

From her glass encased penthouse Lucinda Craven looked over the city and its sprawling suburbs. She wondered where the suburbs ended. She knew it was in the foothills of the mountains, but how long would it be before even those treelines would be decimated to become housing blocks. When it did occur, she wanted to make sure people would be driving home in one of her cars.

Her phone rang.

"What do you mean he has gone missing?" Lucinda asked the head of security.

The response didn't matter, but she waited for him to finish.

"What do I pay you for? Is it to make mistakes?"

"We are certain it didn't happen at our end, we did our best to—"

"You did your best to come up with an excuse? Is that it?

How dare you even call me at this time of night, about something so basic? So avoidable. It's long after midnight. Would you like me to come down there and do your job for you?" blasted Lucinda. Using a spray bottle full of water she sprayed mist on her plants with one hand, holding the phone in the other.

"We checked when the Crash Test Dummies left the factory, they were all there . . ." the head of security tried to explain.

"Your employee number is 6791," Lucinda said, glancing at her computer monitor. "I expect this will be sorted out by morning. Get a patrol car on the road and find him."

"A car has already been sent out," said the head of security.

"I don't care. Send out another. Immediately. Because your plan obviously hasn't worked. Do I make myself clear?"

"Yes, boss. It will be done right away."

"Your employee number has been recorded. All further infractions will see you reprimanded. CrashCorp would not be able to recommend you for further employment at any other institutions. Is that what you'd like?"

"I assure you it didn't happen at our end. We bar-coded all dummies before they went out, and we have the scan to prove he was loaded onto the truck."

"If I could employ people to give me excuses, they would certainly have to come up with better ones than you have," Lucinda said. "Sort it out."

Lucinda hung up the phone.

Treat matters as though trivial and they will soon become that way, Lucinda thought. Lucinda slept soundly, knowing she had put things right.

*   *   *

The CrashCorp security car glided through the streets. The electric engine created almost no sound.

The security guards in the car watched as a police car came towards them in the opposite direction. Crossing paths, the occupants of the cars observed each other.

"Sorting out other people's problems," sneered the CrashCorp driver, noticing a kid huddled up in the backseat. "Look like they've captured another delinquent."

"Boys still playing pretend cops and robbers," said Senior Constable Billing to Grieves.

CrashCorp security patrolled the path the truck had taken. It looped back and systematically scoured the alleyways in the surrounding areas. Their night would be long; shining spotlights in doorways, down alleyways and behind whatever rubbish people had dumped. They scoured every place that could be scoured and all without getting out of their car. Occasionally they would radio back to base to let CrashCorp know they had not found the missing dummy. They stopped for breakfast, long before it was breakfast time. When it was breakfast time, they would stop again.

CrashCorp security didn't see the need to concern themselves too much with finding the dummy escapee.

Several years before, a dummy managed to find itself on the outside of the facility. Venturing no more than a few blocks, unable to resist its natural urge, the dummy found an unlocked car. Shortly afterwards it found an oncoming train. CrashCorp denied any knowledge, which was true as it was unaware the Hybrid was missing. Police reported the matter as a prank, most likely played by teenagers who had stolen the dummy. CrashCorp agreed that their estimation of events was most likely correct. Sebastian's fate would probably be similar. The security guards knew it was just a matter of waiting for a news report to alert them of an accident. Preferably after they had finished their second breakfast.

*   *   *

Emperor Norton jumped from the couch with a *meow* and scurried under the coffee table. Heavy knocking on the front door had startled him. It had also woken Kym. She was not sure what time it was, as the antique grandfather clock in the lounge hadn't been wound in nearly a year. Kym pulled herself out of the armchair and made her way to the door. Fumbling, she flicked on the outside light switch. Light flooded through the glass panels of the front door. Unlatching the deadlock, she left the security chain in place and opened the door only a sliver.

Max stood before her, dwarfed by two officers.

"Mrs Alderson, I am Constable Grieves. We have had an incident with your son."

Kym looked down at Max. Emperor Norton purred around her feet. She lifted him up as she removed the door chain.

"What's happened?" Kym asked. "Why aren't you in bed?"

"I didn't do it," Max shouted, as he pushed passed his mother and ran towards his room.

Kym pulled the front door closed. On the porch, Kym and the police officers talked. The police radio screeched with incoming calls as they explained how they had picked up Max in the industrial estate. Constable Grieves informed Kym that Max could be charged with damaging property.

"Things have been difficult for a while," said Kym.

Sitting on an old couch, Constable Grieves sat beside Kym. Senior Constable Billing stood. They talked under the porch light, as a flutter of moths conducted kamikaze missions into the bulb. Emperor Norton chased the moths once they hit the ground.

Kym explained the recent events and offered some kind of justification for what Max had done. The police informed her they would talk to the business owner in the morning and see if they wished to press charges. When the police left for their next call, Kym made sure Emperor Norton was inside and closed the door. She turned off the light and the moths flew away.

From his bed Max watched the shadows under the door. For a moment his mother's feet hovered outside. Her bedroom door finally clicked shut.

Trying to get a few hours sleep would most likely be futile. Curling under the covers Max tried to forget his embarrassment. He kept thinking about how he freaked out when being driven home in the police car. Listening to his mother's muffled voice talking to the police, he was afraid they were going to break down his bedroom door and take him away. He was glad when everyone decided to leave him alone.

Sleep came. Eventually. Sort of.

06

Max left for school before his mother woke. Something he was glad about. He walked down the alley running along the back of his house and turned into the street, passing the bus stop where other kids from his school waited. He didn't acknowledge anyone and continued walking. He wondered if he should do just that, continue walking, skipping school to see where the day would take him. He was in enough trouble already and decided against it.

The day was a confusing blur. Max spent it moving from one classroom to the next, not remembering much in between the times the bells rang. Almost falling asleep in class, Max's head began to fall forward, before jerking up again. The math teacher noticed and asked him a question.

"It's in Germany," Max responded as he returned to consciousness.

He spoke to few people. During lunch he fell asleep on

the lawn, before being woken by a teacher yelling at him to get to his next class. As much as he looked forward to the final bell, he was also dreading it. It meant he had to return home.

Each step he took up the alleyway he felt heavier and heavier, until he felt like he was sinking. The bluestone paving felt hot, even through the soles of his shoes.

Hearing a whizzing sound Max looked up to see a girl drop from a tree branch. Hanging from a rope, wearing abseiling gear, the girl was suspended before him. She had rough shoulder length black hair and large green eyes. She dangled on the end of the rope like a gigantic Christmas decoration.

"Why don't you catch the bus?" she asked. "It's quicker."

"What the—" Max said.

"What? Never seen a girl fall from a tree before?" she said. "I'm Layla. I go to the same school as you."

Max wasn't quite sure how to respond. He had seen girls fall from trees before; also from monkey bars, school stair railings, bikes, pogo sticks, fences, while dancing on the kitchen table, and from many other places. Usually they fell with a high-pitched scream and landed in an unbecoming position. But this girl just hung there. From a rope. From a tree.

"I saw you walking to school this morning. You walked passed the bus stop with an early morning zombie stare," said Layla, as she dangled. "You crashed out at lunch too."

Max put his hand in his pockets and turned his eyes to the ground. He didn't want to talk about school. He didn't really want to talk. One thing he was sure he didn't want to do was go home.

"And you are?" Layla asked.

"Sorry, I'm Max."

Layla lowered herself to the ground and unclipped her harness.

"Hi, Max. Want to belay me?" smiled Layla. "Or should I belay you?"

Max felt his face become hot as the blood rushed to his cheeks.

"I don't . . . Um . . . I . . ." stumbled Max.

"Belay," said Layla. "It's where we support each other by holding the ropes as the other climbs. That way we won't get hurt if we fall when we lose our grip."

"Oh," said Max. "Okay."

"Are you just going to stand there or come up?" she asked.

Max looked up the tree to see the ropes stretching from an overhanging branch.

"I don't really feel like climbing that. I don't know how."

Layla glanced at Max as though he was an idiot. She opened the back gate and led him into her backyard. Max saw the brick paving that could have been laid there in the Depression era. It jutted out at odd angles and weeds grew through the cracks. The back of the house had been demolished. Plywood and plastic sheets covered large sections of the frame. Sinks and bathtubs and doors and windows and plaster and planks and pipes and wires and handles and floorboards and glass and everything else that could be ripped out of the guts of a house was strewn across the backyard.

Max cast his eyes up.

"Wow," gasped Max. "That's cool."

A large wooden platform made up the floor of the treehouse. The trunks of three trees supported it. The walls were made from old doors and oddly placed windows. Mismatched pieces of timber filled in the gaps, some cut to size, others left hanging over. It was though the treehouse hovered in the branches.

"How come I've never noticed this?" Max said, dumping his backpack on the last remaining section of grass.

"None of it can be seen from the alley. The neighbours don't even know about it. The last thing I want is someone telling me to rip it down just because someone made up some stupid rule that says I'm not allowed to have it."

Layla pulled on a rope that released half an A-frame aluminium ladder. It hit the ground with a clang. The ladder went up to a trapdoor.

"Some of it was already here when we moved in," Layla said, stepping onto a rung. "Actually, it was just a few planks of wood and a piece of old tin as a roof. Mum and dad started renovating, so I just used what they didn't want. I got a bit carried away."

Max followed Layla up the ladder and climbed through the trapdoor. He was amazed he could stand up inside. He reached and touched the roof with the flat of his hand. Looking through a battered French door, now recycled as a window, Max looked towards the back of the house. An old kitchen cabinet lined one wall, stuffed with Layla's things. A mattress filled the floor on the other side, covered by an ancient mosquito net. In the middle of the treehouse a trunk had been built around and the offcut branches used as hooks for Layla to hang her gear. The tree didn't seem to mind.

"You live here?" asked Max.

"You want to see upstairs?"

Max turned as Layla pulled hard on a scarf hanging from the roof. An old wooden door that made up a section of the roof lowered. Wooden slats had been nailed onto it, to make it easier to walk up.

"There's still more," said Layla, her harness jingling as she climbed.

The afternoon sun filled the deck hidden between the treetops. Layla pulled the door up. The roof was made from a jigsaw of old building materials. Odd pieces of timber with the nails removed, with black rust stains, made up the railing around the edges. Leaves and branches covered it from the outside world. If anyone did happen to see their heads poking out, they might simply think it was just a couple of kids climbing a tree. A hammock hung between two braches. A telescope pointed towards the sky.

They looked over the surrounding rooftops and at the distant skyscrapers.

"Which one's yours?" asked Layla.

"That brown tiled roof," Max pointed through the branches. Max thought about what awaited him at home.

He couldn't avoid it forever, but it did seem like a good idea. "I can't believe you're allowed to build this!"

"Didn't have much else to do over the summer holidays. Not like I know anyone yet," said Layla, looking over the view. "Besides, it keeps me out of the way while my folks renovate. That and they're using my bedroom for storage space."

"Have you just moved here?" asked Max.

"Thanks, you didn't even notice the new girl at school."

"I've just started there also."

"You just moved too, that's cool?" Layla said. "Where are you from?"

"Here," Max answered, looking out towards the roof of his house. "Just changed schools."

"Why?"

"Just stuff," mumbled Max, looking away.

"Yeah," sighed Layla. "So, I've got a spare harness downstairs?"

Max followed Layla back into the treehouse. She took a harness from a branch and helped Max into it.

"Wait on the ground," said Layla.

From the deck Layla dropped a coil of rope after securing it, then headed down to Max.

"I'll climb first, you belay." Layla strapped them both into the carabiner and showed Max how to hold the rope. "Only give me enough slack to let me climb, don't try and pull me up. Most important, hold on and stay focused in case I fall."

Layla had fixed a series of coloured holds on the trees

trunks. She climbed only using one colour hold as she went. She reached the top.

"Now lower me down." On the ground Layla unclipped her carabiner. "Your turn."

"Mine?" Max said, his face dropping.

Layla threaded Max up.

"Use any holds you like."

Max began to climb with Layla watching on as she belayed.

"It's okay, you won't splat on the ground," she said. "Unless I want you to."

Max began to climb, unsure how to position his feet and hands. Only a short way up, Max's legs began to tremble and he felt weak. Layla giggled. Max reached for a hold, his fingers barely touching it. He slipped, swinging out from the tree. Max swung like a pendulum, hanging in mid-air. He turned and looked down to Layla, which made him feel worse.

"Can you let me down?" Max's voice shook. "Please?"

Instead of lowering Max, Layla laughed. "Not until you tell me why you don't like the bus."

"I don't *not* like the bus." Max strangled the rope. "I just don't *take* the bus."

"Too good for public transport, hey?" Layla called. "Afraid of us common folk or just spoilt from getting driven everywhere?"

"I just prefer to walk. That's all."

"You're lying, but enough torture. Bombs away." Layla released the rope and lowered a relieved Max to the ground. Breathing deep, he fumbled as he unbuckled his carabiner.

They hung out at the treehouse, and hung off the treehouse, until it became dark. For a while Max's thoughts were not about going home, they had been overpowered by adrenaline as he attempted to climb. Max departed up the alley, pausing to see if he could spot the treehouse. He couldn't. Just a few fairy lights were visible.

Entering through the garage, Max walked up the garden path. He noticed the glow from the kitchen window.

07

Max carefully slid open his bedroom window, edging it just a little at a time. The warm breeze and the sounds of the night flowed through the gap. In the night silence even the slightest movement seemed to rattle the whole house. Max had learnt after his first attempt of sneaking out of the house how to escape without being noticed. He had cleaned the grime from the window runners and wiped them with cooking oil. He had practiced sliding the window back and forth, listening intently for where each point made a sound. The fly wire screen lay against the fence, where it had been for months. Maybe it had fallen. Maybe Max had pushed it out. His mother didn't seem to notice or care. She was tucked up under the sheets with Emperor Norton.

Stepping onto the window ledge, Max eased himself to the ground. Lined with pebbles and a forest of weeds, Max scanned both directions of the space that ran up the side of his house. Leaving through the front yard would mean passing his mother's bedroom window. It could be done, but if his mother lay awake staring at the sky, she would see him. The roller door of the garage would squeal if he tried to open it and sneak down the alley.

Rounding through the back garden, Max made his way up the far side of the house. The path to the padlocked gate was barricaded by stuff that no longer had a place in the house, or hadn't found a place in the garage, but couldn't yet be thrown away. His escape route was blocked by plastic rubbish bins, rusted bikes and broken, sun-faded toys.

Climbing onto the fence, Max pried his fingers between the warped wooden palings. Shuffling along, he passed his sister's window. The lights were off and the pink curtains drawn. He had become an expert at navigating this crossing. He was soon over the gate and making his way through the streets.

Crossing the train lines, Max plotted his way along the backstreets as he had done a few nights earlier. He passed near where the police had apprehended him. He hadn't heard anything from the police since they dropped him home. He had spent his time moving around the house, sharing the same space with his mother, but at the same time avoiding her. She was doing the same to him. They were in a cold war and neither was willing to fire the first shot.

Tracing back over the path where he had fled from the

police, Max found the building where he had tossed his backpack. Climbing on a propane gas cylinder and up a drainpipe, he scraped onto the roof. Inching along on his stomach he retrieved his backpack and went down the way he came.

Max's piece was still there, unfinished. He was glad it hadn't been buffed over and he didn't have to start again. At school Max had gone over his plan many times. So many times he had almost confused himself with the details. Saturday night, tonight, he would complete it. He had seen on the news the police were placing more patrols on the inner city streets to curb drunkenness and a recent spate of violence. Tonight, as his theory went, they would be focused elsewhere, hopefully leaving him alone.

Pumped up with adrenaline, Max shook a can and pressed the nozzle. To him painting was almost like performing. Cutting lines, adding fades and bubbles, highlights and white lining. Max could feel his muscles tensing out of fear of being discovered, but managed to hold the can steady. In less than three hours he was done. Pulling his phone from his pocket, he took a photo, hoping no one would see the flash. He didn't really care too much if anyone did see it, though. It might attract someone to come over and look at his work. People were now welcome to look at it as much as they wanted.

Darting back towards home, the fear and adrenaline turned to unabated excitement. He had finished his first real piece, not counting some quick tags and trials. He almost didn't care if the police caught him again. It didn't matter now, and it wouldn't take long before they realised he had made a second attempt. What could they do? Make him rub it out? This wasn't a sketch on paper anymore. It was real. All he wanted to do now was get home, download the image, and stick a print on his wall. For once he was not worried about making noise. Even the rattling marbles in the spray cans didn't bother him. He didn't need the cans anymore. Besides, most were near empty. In case he was caught again, he decided it would be best to get rid of them.

Lifting the lid of a dumpster, Max emptied the contents of his backpack inside to dispose of the evidence, this time he included his dust mask. Looking up at the stars, he paused to take a few deep breaths. He had done *something*. Something others had to notice. Something people might even consider art. Even if they didn't like it, or considered it vandalism, he had done something. He had expressed himself. He had let the world see part of himself he couldn't show in person. It didn't matter if they liked it or not. It didn't matter if they didn't know he created it. He knew.

Clang.

Max jumped. More than jumped. Threw himself against the opposite wall. Excitement reverted back to fear. He slid over into the shadows, camouflaging himself against the bricks.

A couple of spray cans flew out of the dumpster, bounced on the pavement and rolled towards him. The lid of the dumpster flew up. Old bubble wrap rose like a ghost.

"How did I do?" Sebastian said, pulling the bubble wrap off himself.

"Shhh," hissed Max, stepping out of the darkness. "What are you still doing here?"

"Hiding," said Sebastian, "Pretty impressive, huh?"

"You stayed here the whole time?" asked Max.

"Of course," smiled Sebastian. "In a game of hide-and-seek I once hid for seven months. I crept into the roofing joist of the factory. The only reason they found me was because they were demolishing part of the building. I thought they would be happy when they found me, but they were just angry creatures. Humans are weird."

"Are you insane? Or homeless? Or something?" Max asked.

"Not sure. What do you mean?"

"Don't you have somewhere else to go?"

"Ah, somewhere to go. Of course," said Sebastian. He climbed out of the dumpster, rubbish clinging to his overalls. "I'm going to Elcycer."

Catching his foot on the edge of the dumpster, Sebastian fell to the ground. A rat ran up the length of the bubble wrap hanging from the dumpster.

"Goodbye, Squeaker." Sebastian waved to the rat who had kept him company, as it scurried towards the train line.

Sebastian rose to his feet and pulled off the rubbish.

"What's Elcycer?" asked Max.

"Don't be modest in my presence." Sebastian pressed his grubby hand on Max's shoulder. "Everyone has heard of the Land of Heroes."

"You're a hero?" asked Max, as he covered his nose. "Of what?"

"Some of the best crashes you could imagine. Not just any dummy becomes a hero. Not to my standard, anyhow. It takes years of dedication. Who else do you think tests all these walls to make sure they don't fall down? Who helps develop cars, so you can get lodged in the windscreen with ease? I practically invented how to skewer yourself on a pole."

"Okay?" said Max.

"Sebastian. Crash Test Dummy. Please to meet one of my fans."

"Yeah," said Max, looking around for which direction he could leave.

Hearing the distant sound of screeching car wheels, Max grabbed Sebastian by the sleeve and pulled him towards the darkness of the back lanes.

"We can't stay here. It's not safe."

"Great," said Sebastian. "You can show me the way to Elcycer."

08

On the deck of her treehouse, Layla peered through her telescope at the few stars and planets not blocked out by light pollution. A tripod held the telescope steady as she watched the moons orbiting around Jupiter. The night breeze rustled the branches, mixing with the sounds of the city. She rested in the hammock, dressed in a singlet top and pyjama pants, small bruises covered her legs from rock-climbing. The mattress inside the treehouse was comfortable, but Layla enjoyed the heavy sleep of being in the open air and decided to spend the night on the roof. With her computer on her lap, she searched the interactive night sky maps on the internet to find observable constellations and planets.

A pebble bounced on the deck. She looked across, ignored it, and returned to star gazing. Another bounced on the deck and hit her in the head. Slipping out from under the telescope, she crawled over and spied down through the leafy camouflage to the ground. She saw a figure standing in the alley.

"Max?" Layla whispered loudly.

"Can I come up?" Max spoke up through the trees.

"You do realise I have a bell? You don't have to bombard me with projectiles."

"Sorry," called Max. "Can I just come up?"

"Not until you ring the bell," ordered Layla.

Max pushed open the unlocked gate, and searched around in the small light available. He hunted for a string with a bell attached. He felt along the fence and swiped his hands through the air, hoping to catch a cord. He moved back out to the path.

Max called, "I can't find it."

"Try the button on the nearest tree trunk," Layla replied. "Electricity has been invented."

Opening his eyes wide, Max spotted a wire extending down from the treehouse. He followed until he found the button and pressed it.

"Who is it?" Layla called.

"You know who it is." Without waiting for a response Max answered, "It's Max."

The ladder dropped and clung as it hit the ground. The trapdoor unlocked and opened. Outside fairy lights flashed on, showing Max the way up.

"Max," called Layla, sticking her head through the trapdoor. "What a lovely surprise visit." Max climbed the ladder. As he reached inside the treehouse, Layla was already on her way back up to the roof. He followed.

"What you up to?" said Max.

Layla crawled back onto the hammock and regained her place under the telescope. Max sat down on the deck, looked up and scanned the sky.

"Have you ever wondered how strange it is that we're all made of the same stuff as stars?" Layla said. "The Universe started more than fourteen-billion-years ago and it ended up as us. Everything went in to creating this very moment. We could have been just atoms floating around a star, light-years away from anything. Except we ended up as this squishy human stuff, that makes songs, snot, and talkback radio. Which I guess means we're still a bunch of atoms floating around a star, but you know what I mean. We could've even ended up as bits of a star, or an asteroid, or some animal on another planet, but some how we ended up as us. Pretty cool, huh?"

"I'm just still trying to figure out this planet," Max mumbled.

"Come have a look at this?" Layla signalled for Max to look through the telescope. He settled himself in the hammock next to Layla and positioned his head under the telescope. He watched as the small points of light came into focus. "See Jupiter and the moons around it? Scientists know there's water on Europa and maybe life. Once people thought we were the only planet with water and life, and now they have found water on the moon, Mars and all over the place. Even on some cooler places of the sun."

"You're not going to start telling me about UFOs and crop circles next?" Max asked.

"There has to be something else out there. After all we are made of the same stuff." Layla responded. "What do you think is out there?"

"I have something to show you," said Max. Layla rolled over and glared at him. She could see nervousness in his eyes. "It's downstairs."

"What is?" Layla said, jumping over Max and heading down the stairs. Layla bounded through the treehouse and down the ladder.

"Wait," Max called after her. "I have to tell you something first."

Leaping onto the ground, Layla looked around in the darkened backyard. She glanced around, searching for a gift.

"Where is it?" asked Layla.

Max's feet tumbled down the ladder after her, sliding on the last few steps.

"Well?" said Layla.

Max inhaled deep. "Sebastian."

They waited.

"It has a name?" Layla whispered. "Is it a puppy? There's no way my parents are going to let me keep a puppy. I've tried it before. Twice. And once with a goat."

"It's not an animal. It's not really an *it*. It's more of a thing," said Max. "Sebastian, you can come out now."

From behind the tree trunks Sebastian appeared. He took a step towards them and stumbled, colliding with the fence. Layla darted over to the rubble pile and picked up a broken piece of brick.

"You can't just bring anyone here," Layla shouted. "This is my place, not some neighbourhood club house."

"Just wait," Max pleaded.

Sebastian climbed to his feet and blundered into the glow of fairy lights.

Layla eyed Max warily, "What is he?"

"He's a Crash Test Dummy," Max looked at Layla, unsure. "Apparently. Or completely bonkers. I'm not certain which."

"Is he dangerous?" Layla asked, still holding the brick and ready to fire.

"Only to himself, I think," said Max.

"Another miniature human! How tiny do you guys get?" asked Sebastian.

A glint of anger would have been visible in Layla's eyes if not for the darkness. She knew she was short. Well, short-ish. Not as tall as others. She didn't need reminding by a stranger in her own backyard. She took aim and hit her target. The brick bounced off Sebastian's chest. It dropped to the ground. He didn't even flinch.

Layla's anger subsided and was quickly replaced by awe. She took a closer look at Sebastian. She noticed the pinkish latex skin and crash symbols on his temples. As she observed him, he did the same to her.

"He's either a Crash Test Dummy, or it's one awesome fancy dress costume," she said. "I've heard about these before, but I've never actually seen one."

"You and me both."

"What are you going to do with him?"

"I've absolutely no idea."

"We could take him to the police."

"Yeah, I would rather not do that. I sort of have a thing with police right now."

The inside lights of Layla's house flickered on.

"My parents are home. Get him upstairs," she ordered.

Max sat with Sebastian on the floor of the treehouse as Layla walked around trying to make sense of what was going on. She paced back and forth, ducking her head under a branch as she went. She tried forming sentences in her mind, but stopped herself from saying them, until she found exactly what she wanted to say. She dropped to the floor and sat cross-legged in front of them.

"So you are a—" began Layla.

"A Hybrid III, fiftieth percentile male dummy," Sebastian said. "I am an anthropomorphic test—"

"Shhh . . . quiet voice. My parents may hear," Layla said. "Hang on?"

Layla darted up to the roof and came back with her laptop. In the browser she searched for Sebastian's model. She clicked on one of the results and began to read.

The first Crash Test Dummy was Sierra Sam, invented to test ejector seats on military aircraft, to replace the use of human cadavers. Sierra Stan followed, designed to crash test automobiles. But early Crash Test Dummies proved clumsy, and larger than ninety-five percent of the male population. They inspired an improved version known as the Hybrid I, built in 1971. This design of Crash Test Dummy was known as the 50-percentile model, replicating the height and weight of the average adult male. The Hybrid II proved more advanced, though it could still not mimic what occurs to humans in most accidents, and could only effectively test seat belts.

In 1976 the Hybrid III was introduced, and is the most common and successful Crash Test Dummy ever constructed. Other Crash Test Dummies were designed to form a family, including a female adult, a six-year-old child and a three-year-old.

Max sat quietly listening to the history of Crash Test Dummies. What he really wanted to know was what he should do with a dummy once he had found one.

"Heroes, all of them," glowed Sebastian. "Sierra Sam is the Great Great Grand Daddy of us all. You guys can take me where they are now. They would love to meet you."

"Where are they?" asked Layla.

"Elcycer," said Sebastian. "Everyone knows about Elcycer. It's where everyone goes when they leave the factory. Even you my little soft friends," Sebastian slapped them both hard on the shoulders, causing them to lunge forward. "Ask that . . . thing . . . again where Elcycer is," said Sebastian, pointing to the laptop.

"How do you spell it?" asked Layla.

"Spelling is more of a human thing," said Sebastian.

Layla searched the internet for Elcycer, trying different variations of the word. *Alsiair. El Sire. L Si R.* It didn't help she had never heard of the word before, nor knew the correct spelling, and wasn't even sure it was a real place.

"Nope. Not one hit on anything valuable."

"Maybe it just needs a gentle reminder." Sebastian leant over to hit the side of the laptop. "A little manual persuasion works on all kinds of things."

Layla jerked her computer away with one hand, and blocked Sebastian with the other. She eyed him and he slowly lowered his hand.

"Where did you come from?" asked Max.

"The factory," said Sebastian.

"Which factory?"

"The factory."

"What's the factory called?"

"It's not called anything. It's just the factory. How many factories could there be?"

"Sebastian, you need to give us some hint. At least a name," said Layla.

Sebastian looked confused as he tried to remember. Max had an idea.

"Follow me." Max stood up and led Sebastian up the stairs and onto the roof. "Sebastian, have a look around, see if there is anything you recognise."

Sebastian observed the array of different lights for the first time. He saw streetlights, houses, factories, skyscrapers, airplanes, and car headlights snaking across a massive bridge resting on the horizon.

"Does anything look familiar?" Max asked.

"It's beautiful," said Sebastian, gazing out into this new world. "This place just keeps getting bigger and bigger.

Who would have thought the world goes all the way to the bridge over there?"

"This isn't all," Max glanced up to Sebastian. "This is just one city."

A short yell, almost a war cry, came from behind. Layla's leg flew up. She kicked Sebastian in the small of the back. He launched forward and over the railing. Before Max realised what had happened, there was a dull thump as Sebastian hit the ground. Max glared at Layla in horror, and then peered over the railing.

"Sebastian," Max called. "Are you hurt?"

"Hurt?" Sebastian sat up. "Don't know the meaning of the word."

"What did you do that for?" Max asked Layla.

"I just needed to see if he was real. Let's grab the ropes and have some fun." They both rushed down into the treehouse. Layla began loading herself up with climbing gear. Max clambered down the ladder to the ground. Sebastian wobbled as he rose to his feet and Max helped steady him.

"Are you sure you're not hurt?"

"Seriously," said Sebastian. "What is hurt?"

09

"You're under arrest," a voice sounded.

Max leapt back as he walked down the alleyway. His early morning zombie brain was not ready for anything unexpected, not even Layla jumping out from behind a fence.

"Did you have to?" said Max, annoyed with himself for getting scared.

"Morning, Max."

"You're going to miss the bus."

"I'm keeping you company on the way to school this morning. If I like it, I'll keep it up. Until the weather gets bad, at least."

"Please yourself."

"It beats sitting on the bus surrounded by strangers pretending not to notice each other."

Max had spent the remainder of the weekend at the

treehouse, returning home just before midnight. His house was in darkness. Dinner was waiting for him, still in a box in the freezer. Layla had taught Max the basics of climbing, but she hadn't been able to teach Sebastian much at all. Max was slowly gaining his confidence. The unnatural feeling of being suspended in mid-air had begun to ease. Though the feeling of being able to let go and fall, trusting that someone else was there to support him, would take a while longer to master. Sebastian, on the other hand, liked the idea of falling. And crashing. Both.

"I couldn't get Sebastian to settle down all night," Layla said. "I shouldn't have knocked him over the edge. Think he's addicted to it."

"Where's he now?"

"He was asleep when I left. Thought it was better to leave him. I've tied the ladder up so he can't get out."

"We're going to have to figure out what to do with him," said Max.

"It won't take long until he's discovered at my place. He's not the quietest houseguest. My parents are bound to notice a Crash Test Dummy sooner or later. How about your house?"

"Mum's always home." Max adjusted his heavy backpack. "We'll try and figure out where Elcycer is after school. He's not really given us much to go on."

They both jumped as tyres screeched. Halfway along a zebra crossing a large silver four-wheel drive lurched over them. Shock glued them to the spot. They were so close to being hit that they could feel the warmth of the engine.

Inside the vehicle a man glared down at them, holding a phone to his ear. With a frustrated expression on his face, the man swept is hand across the dashboard in a dismissive wave, signalling for Max and Layla to move off the road.

Darting across to the footpath, they watched as the man shook his head in annoyance and accelerated into the intersection. The rear wheel scuffed over the edge of the roundabout, crushing the plants in the garden bed. Without indicating, he turned the corner and drove away with the phone still to his ear.

"Charming," said Layla.

"Some grown ups are not very grown up," said Max.

*   *   *

Sebastian walked along the morning streets. Because of the Hybrid III's flesh coloured latex skin, designed to look much like that of a human, anyone who saw Sebastian from a distance would easily be confused, thinking he was a bald man in work overalls. It was through closer inspection that they would realise he was something else entirely.

Falling from a window had proven useful after Sebastian found himself locked inside the treehouse. He paused to watch cars pass, hoping to catch a glance of a dummy driving. Instead, he only found humans behind the wheel. This appeared curious to him. He was not used to witnessing humans driving. At the factory workers only travelled around on electric trolleys. It was common knowledge amongst the dummies that humans were not very good drivers. Certainly they were not capable of driving cars with any degree of sophistication or skill. That privilege was reserved for the superior ability of Crash Test Dummies. The dummies had noticed humans would do anything to avoid crashing. When a dummy crashed, the other dummies would cheer and congratulate their colleague. Whereas if a human crashed, which was rare, other humans panicked. They would scramble to clean up the debris and almost pretend as if the crash never occurred.

Sebastian kept a short distance behind Max and Layla. They were the only people outside of the factory who he knew. *Maybe*, he thought, *they really do know where Elcycer is, but they aren't allowed to tell. One of those strange human things.*

He noticed they were dressed in almost identical uniforms. Each morning at the factory the workers would march into work all dressed alike.

They're heading to some factory, he thought, *a factory for miniature humans.*

Sebastian lost sight of the pair as they entered the side gate of the school grounds. Trees blocked his view. Hearing a bell ring, Sebastian caught sight of more students. They all wore the same uniform as they raced through the schoolyard. He could no longer pick out Max and Layla as students scurried in different directions. Some students vanished into buildings. Others rushed down paths and disappeared out of sight. Within seconds the schoolyard was empty.

Wandering slowly through the grounds, Sebastian had no idea where to start looking for his friends. The low grumbling roll of an engine sounded, and the faint unforgettable smell of exhaust fumes drew his attention.

Rounding the back of a shed, Sebastian noticed a red ride-on lawnmower. It was not something Sebastian had tried before. Four wheels and a steering wheel, it could only serve one purpose. Sebastian moved towards it. This would be his first opportunity to crash in the outside world.

Approaching the mower, he noticed the shed door was open. Inside a large human was bent over, rummaging through a toolbox. Finding a stick on the ground, Sebastian forced down the roller door, with a loud cascading rattle. He wedged the stick into the space between the door and the overhang, preventing it from being opened. The door rippled as the large human tried to lift it. With his fists, he banged. With his feet, he kicked. With his mouth, he swore. With his whole being, he knew he was trapped.

Smiling to himself, Sebastian climbed on the mower. He felt the machine vibrate through his body. He enjoyed being in the driver's seat once again after spending so long on his legs. Sebastian pushed his foot on the accelerator and was away.

*   *   *

Max sat in his homeroom as the teacher conducted the morning roll call. He had just made it in before the second warning bell rang. Staring out the window he waited for the first class to begin. He watched as the groundskeeper emerged from behind the utilities building, riding a lawnmower across the hockey field. Turning to the teacher, Max answered as his name was marked off.

Rewind.

Replay.

What had he just seen?

Whipping his head around, Max looked back out the window. He watched the mower trail off. His heart did a double beat. That wasn't the groundskeeper.

The teacher finished roll call. Max sat stunned. His eyes darted back and forth as he tried to think of what to do.

"I have a few announcements to make," said the teacher. "First, I have been asked by the principal to remind you that electronic devices can only be used for—"

Max jumped up from his chair.

"I've got to go to the toilet."

"It can wait, Max."

"I don't think it can." Max clutched his books and headed towards the door. "I think I'm about to explode like an upside-down volcano."

The teacher lowered her page of daily announcements as Max rushed across the room. The class erupted in laughter.

"If it's that bad, I want you to see the nurse. I will be checking," she called.

Racing down the corridor, Max dumped his books on top of his locker. Outside, he leapt down the stairs and bolted around the side of the building. Pausing, he listened for the sound of the engine. Across the field he noticed a wonky mown strip of grass and followed the path Sebastian had left.

Max felt the desire to run in the opposite direction as he noticed the trail disappeared through a hole in the hedge. Thin branches, stripped-bare of leaves, lay almost flattened against the ground. They wavered as they attempted to resurrect themselves. Reaching the hedge, Max watched Sebastian and the lawnmower careen down a slope and through a freshly established garden bed. It was disastrous and beautiful at the same time. The mower spat out thousands of mulched up flower heads, which fell in a colourful rain.

Without attempting to find the brake pedal, Sebastian crashed into the side of the gym. The rear wheels of the mower lifted off the ground on impact. Sebastian's body flung forward, crumpling against the bricks. He fell to the ground as the mower rolled on top of him.

Max ran towards the mangled machine. He was unable to get closer until the blades jutted to a stop. His eyes searched for any sign of movement. Sebastian's twisted leg protruded from under the wreckage.

Slowly a hand rose up against the wall and clasped the seat. With the scraping of metal, the mower was pushed forward. Max ran up and helped pull it off Sebastian.

"What the hell are you doing?" screamed Max.

"Max, you have got to try this," Sebastian said, excited, pushing the mower clear. "Just after I have one more turn."

"No, you're not," yelled Max.

Max grabbed Sebastian by the hand and dragged him away. Soon the teachers would be searching the school. With something like this occurring, the whole school would be out for a gawk. Nothing could stop a herd of teenagers once they began to move en masse with an intense desire to graze on their curiosity.

Max led them both along the trees running against the back fence. Checking to make sure they couldn't be seen, Max helped Sebastian over the fence and into a vacant allotment. He hesitated as he tried to think of where he could take Sebastian. He considered taking him home, though his mother would be there. Even if he could hide Sebastian in the garage, it would still be risky.

Max ran, hauling Sebastian behind him. They darted through the back streets.

From the alley, he peered over the fence into Layla's backyard. There was no sign of her parents. Max unlocked the gate after flipping himself over the fence.

"You humans really have got to learn the art of crashing. It is so much fun."

"Get in," Max barked, yanking on Sebastian's arm.

Frustrated, Max untied the ladder and dragged Sebastian up into the treehouse.

"You hide here. Don't come out," Max ordered, his voice shaking.

Unsure what to do, Max rested in the alley for a few minutes. He could run off for the day, or maybe longer. The police would soon be after him as he was already on their radar. He could tell the truth: a Crash Test Dummy was responsible. He was only trying to prevent the catastrophe, but even Max had trouble believing what had really happened. Max decided he would return to school and revert to what he labelled as his "shut down mode".

Max felt heavy with despair as he turned to approach the school gates. He spotted the principal speaking to his mother. Her arms were folded across her chest. Angry stance. His mother's glare locked on him. Followed by the principal's. They were both ready to fire.

10

Max sat with his mother in the principal's office, refusing to speak. Of course, he knew no matter what he said, the blame would still land on him. Once an adult made up their mind about something they usually stuck with it, especially if other adults agreed. At least if he tried to explain to someone his own age they would demand to see proof of Sebastian, instead of dismissing him outright. Most people had heard of Crash Test Dummies, or watched videos of them crashing, but their containment was generally tightly controlled. Their presence in the human world was incredibly rare that most people wouldn't consider it a possibility they were in the outside world amongst them.

"Max, if you're not going to talk, I want you to leave my office so I can speak to your mother." Principal Garvin stared at Max over the frames of his glasses. Kym gave him a weak obliging smile.

Max gladly left. He sat on the hard plastic chairs in the waiting area, with his arms crossed and legs bouncing nervously. He knew what they were talking about. His mother would be going over why Max had left his last school. How the last year had been difficult. How Max had been acting out. Explaining how efforts were being made to get him back on track, and all they needed was a little more time.

Max waited, glancing through the frosted glass office door. Time dragged. He wondered how they could find so much to talk about. Students walked by in pairs, watching Max waiting, hoping to catch a glimpse of the unfolding drama. They would talk, construct a patchwork story, and create their own versions about what had occurred. Each version would be slightly more elaborate than the last. None would be right. Max had already resigned himself to this. It didn't matter what school he went to, the kids were all the same.

The office door eventually clicked open.

"Make sure you send me a quote for the damage, Principal Garvin."

"I will let you know when we have one ready, Mrs Alderson."

Principal Garvin gave Max a stony glare. Max knew everything in front of him was uncertain once more.

"Good bye, Principal Garvin," Kym said, unsure if she should shake his hand. She decided not to, feeling much like she was back in her own school days. Turning, she flashed Max an angry glare. She grabbed him by the arm, dragged him out of the chair and led him out into the hallway.

"Get your bag," she demanded.

A pack of girls looked at each other as gossip pooled in their eyes.

Max's feet didn't stop as his mother forced him off the school grounds. The heat was already rebounding off the footpath. Max was moved along, just like he had done to Sebastian only an hour earlier. He didn't speak. Intuitively he knew he shouldn't say anything until his mum did first.

"You're lucky you weren't expelled," yelled Kym, dry spit flying from her mouth. "He would have if I didn't talk him around. He wanted to call the police. How do you think that is going to look? One week's suspension. Bloody hell, Max. And I had to waste money on a taxi fare here."

"Mum, I didn't mean—" Max started.

Kym stopped and pointed her finger right in Max's face. "Don't you even . . . I don't know how much this is going to cost me. I don't know how you are going to pay me back. But, you are."

Clutched by his arm, Max was wrenched forward. He felt as if the summer heat could melt him right onto the footpath as he was marched home.

*   *   *

A haze of bright afternoon sun filtered around the edges of the drawn curtains as Max hid himself in his bedroom. He sketched rapidly in a notebook. None of the drawings were any good. All were rushed in a wave of anger and emotion. He didn't know what he was trying to draw. He just needed a distraction. Headphones pumped music into his ears as the television flickered light across the darkened room.

The door slowly opened. Max swallowed as he focused harder on his drawings. His lines became rougher and heavier. His mother entered and appeared nervous. Even though Max didn't look at her, he could tell by the way she approached that she was uncomfortable about something. Sitting on the end of his bed, Kym clutched an envelope.

Max ignored her.

Gently, Kym placed her hand on Max's leg. He pulled it away. Taking a deep breath Kym folded the envelope in her hand. Wiping her hair from her face, tucking it behind her ears, she turned to Max. Max could tell she was saying his name, and asking to speak to him. All he could hear was music. She made a few attempts before her face fell and she looked towards her knees.

Snatching the cord, Kym ripped the headphones from Max's ears.

"You're going to talk to me."

"Yeah, right," Max grumbled, turning towards the wall.

"This has got to stop," said Kym. "It's not all about you. Have you thought about what your behaviour might be doing to others? How it might be affecting me?"

Kym waited for a response. Max stared blankly at a printout of his graffiti he had stuck to the wall. Kym knew a response would not be forthcoming.

"Max?" Kym said softly.

Max knew he should say something to make his mum feel better. He just didn't know what to say. He pulled his legs up close to his chest.

"Max. This isn't just going to go away. We need to start dealing with this. And I can't do it without you," Kym's voice began to waver.

Max reached for the television remote, pressed the mute button to bring the sound back on, and turned up the volume. Kym took a few deep breaths as she had practiced. As calmly as she could she walked over to the television and turned it off. Max pressed another remote and turned on the stereo. In frantic anger she pushed buttons until she killed the music.

Kym threw the envelope at Max. It landed on his chest.

"That's a summons to appear in court," Kym yelled. "If you want to deal with this yourself, you go right ahead. Try it. Support is a two way street. Maybe you don't know how to handle it. Well, guess what? Maybe I don't know how to handle it either." Max noticed tears fall down her cheeks. "Why can't I just have my boy back?"

The door shook the whole house as she slammed it closed. Max grabbed the remote control and turned the television back on. A commercial about a new model of electric car played, which had a special kind of paint to capture solar energy and a fuel cell that recharged itself as it drove. It never needed to be refuelled. The car flashed across the screen and the advertisement ended, becoming lost in the multitude of others that followed.

Max grabbed his headphones and pushed them back in his ears. The music blocked out the world. He let himself drift away.

11

Layla had been distracted all day as she tried to piece together what had happened with Max. Girls and gossip surrounded her like a cyclone. Boys moved in packs, one always making a comment loud enough for her to hear. In class they sat in their cliques and pelted her with questions.

"Why did he trash the school?"

"Is he a psycho?"

"I read online he was kicked out of his old school for attacking a teacher. And she died."

"Are you two going out together?"

"You were both expelled from your last school, weren't you? You can tell me."

All day. All. Day.

In class Layla was thankful when the teacher spoke. It meant for a brief time she would be left alone. For some reason, possibly group hysteria, everyone assumed Layla knew everything about Max: his every thought, everything he did, or had done. They seemed annoyed she could not read his mind. Whatever questions they asked, Layla was hardly going to give them a truthful answer. She wasn't going to satisfy them by explaining that she only knew a little more about Max than any one else did. Usually, it took a while for anyone to start talking to her after she changed schools. In other circumstances, Layla might have been grateful. But, now she just wished they would all shut up.

When she found a moment to herself, she sent a text to Max. She received nothing in reply. Almost immediately the quiet moment disappeared and Layla started deflecting questions catapulted her way.

"Is it true he stole a car and drove it into a crowd?"

"My friend used to go to school with him and said . . ."

The final bell was the sound of relief. With her bag slumped over her back, Layla left school, swamped in a sea of gossiping kids.

Pulling down the ladder to her treehouse, Layla popped her head through the trapdoor.

Sebastian sat waiting.

"You're here?" she said blankly. "So, it wasn't you?

"I have the best news to tell you." Sebastian jumped up. "Where's Max? He can also tell you all about it."

"About what?" Layla kicked the trapdoor closed.

"That place you go to. It's so much fun. I can see why you go."

Layla threw her bag against the wall.

"I went for a ride on this plant chopper-thing," Sebastian beamed. "I've never experienced anything like it."

"Stop," yelled Layla.

"It was spectacular. Not only does it drive. It demolishes everything in its path. Pure awesomeness."

"Stop."

Ripping the ties from her hair, she pushed Sebastian against a branch running up through the treehouse. Seeing the fun of being pushed, he went to push her back.

"Touch me and you're dead," said Layla.

Sebastian looked confused. "Dead? What's dead?"

"Do you know how much trouble Max is in because of you?"

"But, we had fun."

"Fun? You have a warped view of fun."

"What could be more fun? Chopping plants. Crashing. Double fun. Double awesomeness."

"Just shut up," Layla screamed. She pushed her hand hard against her forehead. Taking a deep breath, she steadied her voice. "Have you seen Max this afternoon?"

Sebastian shook his head cautiously. He had seen humans act this way before, when he was in the factory. It was right after he commandeered a forklift and drove it through the wall of their office. All the humans inside had looked bored and he wanted to give them a bit of excitement. They were not happy then, either. He concluded humans didn't understand fun.

"We're going to have to work out how to clean up all this mess," Layla said.

"We don't clean up stuff. That's what the other people do," said Sebastian.

The punch in Layla's eyes knocked Sebastian back into silence.

"Stay here. Don't make a sound. Don't go anywhere. I'm going up to the roof. I need time alone to think." Layla pulled down the ramp, climbed up and pulled it closed behind her.

Sebastian felt as though he had done something wrong. It was an awkward feeling for a Crash Test Dummy, as crashing had ever only brought him praise. He slumped down into the corner and sat quietly. Looking at the door he heard the latch move into place. He was shut out. Isolated in a world that didn't recognise him as a hero, and where for the first time in his life he didn't feel popular.

On the deck, Layla took out her phone and sent Max another text.

Come ova. I think u & Seb need 2 talk.

The beep of Max's reply came.

Not my prob. Neva really was. Hav my own stuff to deal wif.

"What?" Layla stared at the message. Dialling Max, she heard the automatic voice explain his phone was "switched off or not in service".

Collapsing into the hammock, Layla closed her eyes and listened to the gentle roar of the city. The stress of the day had finally drained her energy.

Hearing the sound of her mother calling, Layla woke from a doze. As she walked down through her treehouse, Sebastian looked at her like a dog that knew he was in trouble. He almost spoke, but Layla turned and gave him a quick-draw point of her finger. Nestled in the corner, Sebastian watched the sky turn from orange to a deep blue, until it completely surrounded him in darkness.

After dinner Layla returned. It had given her time to think. She was glad for the short time she could be normal for a change. Her parents had not heard about the day's events. They undoubtedly would as the news travelled along the parental grapevine, and she was getting herself mentally prepared for the eventual confrontation. So far they didn't even know about Max, but she would be dragged into the trouble through association.

Sebastian watched as the trapdoor slowly opened. Layla climbed through the darkness and switched on the fairy lights.

"We need to talk," she said.

They sat together with their legs hanging over the deck. The pale yellow moon pushed its way over the horizon. She began explaining how things worked in the human world.

"When there is an accident, we need to find out why it happened. Accidents are something we try to avoid."

Sebastian appeared to be listening, though Layla wondered if she was actually getting through to him. "Everything you do has a consequence. If not for you, then for someone else. What you did today has a consequence for Max. He has to pay for what you did. And because of that, it has a consequence for us, too."

"How do we fix it?" said Sebastian.

"I don't know. That's what we've got to try and figure out."

They both looked over the suburban lights and talked. Layla explained how they had to keep Sebastian hidden until they were certain of what to do with him. She explained how the stars were made of the same things that made everything else. She explained how Sebastian wasn't crashing into walls to see if they fell down, but rather he was crashing into them to see if the cars would stand up. She explained how the emotional circuitry of humans was even more complex than the electronic circuitry of a Crash Test Dummy.

The moon was almost above them by the time they had finished talking.

"I have to sleep now," said Layla.

Layla fell asleep in the hammock. A restless Sebastian tried to sleep on the deck. It wasn't just the hard timber boards that were uncomfortable, but also something else deep inside of him. He just wasn't sure what it was.

12

Sleepy eyed, Layla woke to what had already been a long week, and there was still two days of school left. She dropped from her treehouse, stumbled through the garden and entered the house for breakfast. She enjoyed the first few moments of wakefulness, before the reality of yesterday's events resurfaced. She had told Sebastian about life in the outside world. She explained the rules about living at her place. Going near the house was out of bounds. Going anywhere near her parents was much further out of bounds.

The house was empty as Layla showered and dressed for school. Her parents were either already at work, or they had planned one of their regular scavenging expeditions through demolition yards, searching for that perfect piece to add to the house. Layla sat on the bare floorboards of the partly renovated house and enjoyed the quiet, hoping the worst of yesterday's events were over.

When she finished her toast, she typed Max a text as she went outside.

We hav 2 catch up. Like it or not. Even if i hav to hunt U down.

Send.

About to place her foot on the ladder, Layla realised she had not seen Sebastian in the treehouse. She used her head to lift the trapdoor and peek inside, which confirmed her fears. Her eyes darted around the backyard. She spotted Sebastian hanging on the clothesline that ran off the shed. Layla's mother's bras were looped over the wire, holding Sebastian up under the armpits. Her father's underwear was draped over his head. He was asleep, quietly snoring. Picking up a stone, she threw it at him. Nothing. She picked up another.

With a stick, Layla lifted the Y-fronts off Sebastian's head.

"What do you think you're doing?" she said.

"Good morning, miniature person."

"You shouldn't be down here."

"Sleeping lying down is just a little too weird. I don't know how you humans do it. It's so unnatural."

Reaching up, Layla unclipped the bras. Sebastian slumped from the clothesline and let his feet regained their balance.

"Upstairs. Now. You're lucky no one saw you." Layla grabbed his hand and she took him inside. Pressing on Sebastian shoulder she lowered him to the floor, where they both sat.

"We have to try and make things right with Max. I'm going to meet him today."

"Great, I can't wait to see him."

"You can't. This is about consequence. You do something wrong, it changes things. Max doesn't want to see you."

Sebastian looked down at the floor. "But, he's my friend."

"If you're going to be friends, you have to act like a friend. Yesterday wasn't friendly."

"What do you mean by not friendly?" asked Sebastian.

"You hurt him."

Sebastian didn't understand.

Layla reached up to the side of Sebastian's head and peeled away one of the black and yellow crash stickers that had started to unglue. She held it on the end of her fingers and showed Sebastian.

"Am I falling apart?"

"Not quite," said Layla.

"Am I turning into a human?"

"I don't think you have to worry about that." Layla stuck the sticker on the tree trunk.

Beep. Beep. A text came through.

i will meet U @ the mall afta U get off skool. Keep Seb away from me.

"What's that?" Sebastian asked.

"Nothing. Gotta go to school."

"What about that uniform-thing?"

78

"It's sports day. I'll be back this afternoon. You'll have to stay here. Don't break anything. If you're good I'll throw you off the roof when I get back."

Layla grabbed her sports kit, leaving her usual bag and laptop behind. She raised the ladder, tied a rope to the end and flung it over a branch. Securing the rope, she locked Sebastian in the treehouse.

*   *   *

Max sat on the steel seat in the mall, flipping his skateboard nervously under his feet. His eyes darted around, searching for where Layla would be approaching. His head was already sinking in a swirl of thoughts about what he would say.

"What am I supposed to do with him?" Layla's voice came from behind.

"You?" said Max. "I'm the one in trouble here."

"Oh, great. Things get a bit messy so you dump him on me. You're the one who found him. How am I going to explain to my parents I have a six-foot tall Crash Test Dummy living in my treehouse?"

"What am I meant to do with him? Leave him at the Crash Test Dummy shelter?"

"So you just run away when you can't be bothered dealing with it anymore?"

"Why are you yelling at me?" said Max.

"I can't stay calm all the time. I'm not the Dalai Lama."

"What would you know about anything? I wish I could

be like everyone else. Just go around living their lives, but I can't. This isn't fun for me. I'm in trouble with the cops. I'm in trouble with school. Everything else is just—"

Max's face turned red. His knuckles whitened around the trucks of his skateboard. Layla saw Max's eyes switch across to a shop front window, housing mannequins behind the glass. In the mannequins faces Max saw a row of Sebastian's looking back at him.

Layla predicted what Max was about to do next.

"Max. Don't."

Layla gripped his forearm, hoping he would relinquish. He let his hand fall, instead of launching his skateboard into the window. Max began to shake, his eyes not knowing where to look.

"Max? What's really going on?"

Screeching of wheels pierced through the mall. In unison everyone stopped and turned. Blue smoke trailed from the bus tyres, leaving behind short black skid marks. Someone had been hit.

*   *   *

"Oracle of Knowledge tell me where Elcycer is?" Sebastian bellowed as he held up Layla's laptop in the air. He hadn't the slightest chance of getting the information out of it. He hadn't the slightest idea of how to use it. Sebastian had grown anxious from waiting. He had grown even more desperate to find Elcycer now he had fallen out with Max. He didn't know if his human friends would help him anymore. The treehouse was lonely when the miniature humans were not around, and he only had the quiet emptiness of the day to keep him company.

Sebastian stood and looked out the window. Through the gently swaying leaves, he caught glimpses of the city. The heat of the day was already beginning to rise, lifting small water-like mirages into the air, hovering so the skyscrapers appeared wavy. Sebastian imagined the other dummies when they reached Elcycer. He envied their excitement at witnessing the endless fields of race circuits, crash zones, crumpled cars, and gigantic piles of wreckage. They would have now met with other Crash Test Dummies, some who they had only heard about in stories, some close to Godlike. Besides, Jupiter would be waiting for him. Sebastian wanted to be there to welcome all the other dummies after they graduated.

"Someone out there must know who I am. And they will know where Elcycer is," Sebastian said to himself.

Sebastian tried to push open the window but found it locked. He scanned around and pulled down the door to the deck. He launched himself over the edge of the railing, bouncing off a branch as he dropped to the ground. He wasn't sure in which direction he needed to head, or where exactly he currently was, but he knew that everyone sought Elcycer as a destination. Everyone longed to enter. Destiny called them. If he asked enough humans, someone would show him the way.

Sebastian developed a theory. Elcycer would be full of cars, as there would be plenty needed for everyone to crash. So, if he followed where most of the cars were driving, they would lead him there. Through the networks of streets he followed cars as they sped by. He chased them down streets and roads and avenues and lanes and across a bridge, until he found himself on a highway.

Walking on the hard shoulder of the highway, Sebastian looked just like any other slightly crazed bald human walking where he shouldn't be walking. He followed the cars into a car park surrounded by a large series of buildings.

Crossing the car park, Sebastian noticed all the different makes of cars. He attempted to open the doors of a few, to take one for a test drive, but found all the cars locked. Yanking a handle sounded an alarm. No one paid any attention.

Sebastian headed towards the mall. He became overwhelmed by the mass of people charging one way or the other.

"What are you selling?" asked an old lady. "You look very fancy."

"I'm looking for Elcycer," answered Sebastian.

"Is that the mobile phone place? Stupid things they are. It's over there, I think. Near the . . . um . . ." the old lady's hand shook as she pointed across the shopping centre road.

Heading in that direction, Sebastian's leg twisted on the gutter. He stumbled onto the road. The grill of a bus bore down on him. Sebastian looked up and smiled.

The impact flung Sebastian through the air for several

metres of pure joy. He crashed landed with a delightfully sickening smack.

Sebastian wondered if perhaps he had found Elcycer after all.

Clasping the steering wheel, shock had already begun to set in for the bus driver. With his mouth hanging open, he forgot to breathe. He looked down to the body sprawled on the road. The driver knew instantly something wasn't right, as there were no signs of movement. One leg had been severed just below the knee and had come to rest a little way from the body. Surviving such an impact was highly unlikely. Even if the victim did survive, with the injuries sustained, the driver didn't know if the person would be lucky or not.

On the inside the bus driver was panicking, but on the outside he was a human statue, caught in a moment of terror. People gathered on the footpath. They stared in horror, no one quite sure what to do.

"Are you okay?" The old lady hunched over to look at Sebastian. "You took quite a wallop. I've got some aspirin in my bag."

Twisting his head around, Sebastian repositioned it with a sharp crack. Leaning on his arms, Sebastian dragged himself over to his leg. Sitting up, he shoved it back into place. He rolled his ankle a couple of times. All seemed to work fine.

From watching in horror, the witnesses gasped in horror. Followed by screams of horror. The bus driver leapt from the cabin. Standing on the road, he watched

Sebastian clamber to his feet. The driver ran. So did many others.

13

Max burst through the crowd as people fled the scene. Clutching his skateboard in one hand, he grabbed Sebastian with the other. Sebastian lurched as Max kept running, leading him through the stationary cars. Layla helped push him towards a lane running between the shops. Reaching the other side of the buildings, Max turned to Sebastian.

Lifting his skateboard, Max swung it, colliding with Sebastian's head. Blows rained down as Sebastian tried to protect himself from the edge of the board. Sebastian knew he didn't understand human behaviour, but he knew what was coming from Max was pure rage. Each hit produced a flat hollow sound.

"Stop," Layla yelled, stepping between them both.

"What goes on inside your head?" said Max.

Sebastian was confused. As far as he knew, inside his

skull was just an empty cavity.

Blood vessels in Max's neck bulged. Sweat beaded on his red face. Dropping his skateboard, he pushed off.

"Where are you going?" yelled Layla.

"Away from him," Max grunted, turning back to see Sebastian slouched and cowering.

"What am I meant to do?"

"Drive him off a cliff for all I care."

"You're the one who found him."

"Well, I wish I didn't."

Sirens from police cars, or an ambulance, or both, sounded in the distance and grew louder as they approached. The night Max found Sebastian flashed through his mind.

The murmur of the growing crowd could be heard as the confusion set in. Raised voices broadcasted across the car park as witnesses signalled which way the trio had ran. The sirens cut off as the vehicles entered the mall.

"Quick." Max motioned for Layla and Sebastian to follow.

Hurrying through the gate, they arrived back at Layla's place. Sebastian had taken a much longer route to the mall, as it was only a few blocks away. They didn't spot any police cars on their way home.

"Do your parent's use this?" asked Max, opening the door of the garden shed.

"Nope," said Layla. "Most tools and things are kept in what should be my bedroom."

Max guided Sebastian inside.

"Sebastian," said Max. "Look, I'm sorry for hitting you. I shouldn't have done that. I'll make it up to you. We are going to play a game. You like games, right?"

Sebastian nodded his head.

"We're going to play hide-and-seek. You hide first. We'll forget where you are, then we'll try and find you again."

"Okay," said Sebastian.

Closing the door, they listened as Sebastian shuffled around to find a place to hide. Max moved the sliding bolt lock across.

"Do you have a padlock?" Max asked Layla.

"My room."

Max followed Layla inside. Some sections of the house looked finished, with others looking as though they were waiting for the builders to return.

"I just need a break from Sebastian. He's driving me crazy," said Max, following Layla up the stairs. A makeshift banister ran up the staircase, which wobbled when touched.

"You're not the only one. Society needs protecting from him," said Layla.

"So this is why you live in a treehouse," said Max, looking around what resembled a building site rather than a bedroom. Bare plasterboards covered only the wall adjoining the upstairs bathroom. The other walls stood uncovered, revealing the wooden frames and cabling. A light fixture hung out of a hole in the ceiling, suspended by electrical wires.

Layla dragged a large metal toolbox across the plywood

floor. She unclipped the latches and rummaged around through the trays of tools.

"This is the third bedroom I've had like this. My parents have a renovation bug. Do them up and sell 'em. My room usually just ends up full of building junk. The only time it looks any good is in the selling brochure, and then it's time to move again."

Max stepped over to a large cardboard box, which looked like it had barely survived the past couple of moving trips. He took out a large trophy with both hands and pulled away the old newspaper wrapping. He held up a multi-tiered trophy ornamented with gold-coloured plastic figurines. Three columns stood about a metre high. Many other trophies remained buried in the box.

"What are all these?"

"Old pageant trophies from when I was a kid. Put them away, they're embarrassing."

Max found a photo frame with cracked glass. Layla wore a blue and white embossed dress, big blonde hair, make-up and a plastic smile. She was a young child that was somehow mutating into an adult.

"That's you?" said Max. "You were a child beauty pageant queen?"

"That's my mum's fault. She used to take me all over the country to perform. Pageants, shopping malls, country fairs, school plays, talent shows, everywhere. She even made me dance in front of strangers at train stations. Every humiliating opportunity to get attention.

"And there were other mums just like her. All competing

us against each other, like horses at an equestrian. All for some stupid tacky trophy. Once we were heading to a show and mum spotted another parent's car on the freeway and she started gunning it. She almost ran people off the road. Didn't care. We had to get there first. We had to win. I thought we were going to die. After we beat them off the freeway, and skipped a few red lights, they caught up to us at a train crossing. I was in tears. Mum looked at me and screamed, 'What the hell is the matter with you?'"

"I can't wait to meet your mum," said Max. "She sounds crazy." He looked closer at the picture. "You had blonde hair and blue eyes."

"Dye and contacts," said Layla. "For a seven-year-old, right?"

Layla left the toolbox and dug down through the trophies. She pulled out a CD and a portable stereo. She plugged in the stereo, loaded the CD and pressed play.

"Ok, today I am singing a song of my own composition. It's called *Pretty, Pretty Girl*."

"Have you seen a pretty, pretty girl?
A pretty, pretty girl like me?
Have you seen a pretty, pretty girl?
Who sings like the birds in the trees?"

Max looked on in stunned amusement, not sure how to react to a girl he had met hanging out of a tree now dancing around like a clockwork doll. Each movement painfully rehearsed, bending and twisting in unnatural ways to show how bright and happy she could act. Her face contorted with exuberant expressions of joy.

"Have you seen a pretty, pretty girl?
A pretty, pretty girl like me?
See her face, see her smile,
As cute as cute as can be.

"Have you seen a pretty, pretty girl?
A pretty, pretty girl like me?
Hair like sunshine, skin so fair,
Eyes as blue as the sea.

"Have you seen a pretty, pretty girl?
A pretty, pretty girl like me?
Yes, you've seen a pretty, pretty girl,
The pretty, pretty girl is me!"

Layla ended her performance with jazz-hands, followed by a curtsy and wave.

Max dropped to the floor, laughing.

"That was great. You should still do pageants." He clapped, not bothering to contain his rolling laughter.

"When I was eleven, which is practically old age in pageant years, we were banned after I secretly changed my routine and sung *Perfect* by Alanis Morissette." Layla returned to working her way through the toolbox. "Didn't go down very well. Almost started a riot with the other mums. I didn't know eyeliner and hairspray could be lethal weapons. Mum didn't talk to me for months. I was happy, but she acted like she lost a child."

Layla threw Max a heavy padlock. He caught it and followed her downstairs.

"After our big finale, I let my hair grow back natural and vowed never to wear dresses or coloured contacts again."

At the shed, Max double checked the sliding bolt and secured the padlock. Resting his forehead on the shed door, he gave a deep sigh of relief.

14

Max pulled open the aluminium sliding door at the back of his house, drew back the dust embedded curtains, and let Layla enter.

"I'm not going to apologise, it's just the way it is."

"That's a lot of stuff." Layla's jaw dropped.

She took a step inside, her feet crunching on the packaging of a portable greenhouse. She cast her eyes over the mounds of mess, stacked to create a maze of paths through the house. Every surface was piled high with one thing upon another. A stale stench filled the air.

Layla wanted to move forth, but didn't know where to put her feet. Grabbing the side of an overfilled bookshelf she turned to Max.

"I think you might need to show me the way. I didn't bring my rock climbing gear."

Max walked carefully through the lounge. He knew just

the right places to step and took Layla's hand to steady her.

Surfaces in the kitchen were non-existent. Dishes, food packets and bottles covered the benches. Somewhere, now lost underneath it all, was a kitchen his father had taken pride in building. A cascade of yellow and brown spills dripped down the cupboard doors, a testament to past meals. The floor was patterned with a brown and blackish film that had trapped dust and cat fur. The wall tiles had collected their own splattered grimy texture. Food containers, breakfast cereal boxes and food processing equipment all gathered around each other.

Layla could see a pathway towards two armchairs pointing at the television. The dust made her sneeze. The smell of old milk cartons almost made her vomit.

Max had become immune to the pong long ago. Scented garbage bags piled up, some with the contents spilling out. Utensils lay encrusted with food, providing a home to bacteria. The inside of the fridge was something best left unseen. Newspapers hid themselves under clock parts, surrounded with busted toys and broken photo frames. The curtains had been closed so long that their hooks had given up, letting shards of sunlight spear through the room, reflecting off the dust in the air. The carpet was still there, somewhere. A feature wall stood half completed, slowly decaying with the rest of its surroundings.

"Careful," Max said. He guided Layla over a pile of old magazines. Down the hall Layla knocked her knees on an old air conditioner.

"Whose room is this?" Layla asked, as they passed a

door.

"Ruby's. My sister. Mines here."

Max pushed open the wooden door. His room was a mess, but compared to the rest of the house it was a haven.

"Welcome to my humble abode," said Max with a fake smile. "It's not what you expected, hey?"

"I didn't expect anything," said Layla. "I can't really judge. Technically, I don't even have a room."

Max jumped onto his bed and switched on the television. Layla sat on the end of his bed. She couldn't stop herself from looking around. Her eyes moving from object to object. Every corner was filled with something different.

"Where did you get all this stuff?" said Layla. "It's interesting. My parents always want to do everything so minimalistic and bland. It's like when a new trend happens they throw everything out just to replace it. I can't see why we have to keep making so much new stuff when there's already plenty on the planet."

"I guess adults like impressing each other. Do you want to watch something?" said Max. "I've downloaded heaps."

"Sure," said Layla. "But can I meet your sister first. She home?"

Without saying anything, Max took Layla down the hallway. Almost tripping over a rusted coffee machine and a dead pot plant, he took her to Ruby's door.

Flicking on the light, Ruby's pink room glowed. Fairy lights hung around the window, love heart lamps stood beside her bed, and a star shone above her princess bedspread. Fairy wings hung over the bed frame.

"Isn't she here?" Layla said. "Does she live with your dad?"

"She's dead," said Max. "So is dad."

"I'm so sorry," said Layla.

They stepped inside the room. Everything was clean and organised. Not a thing out of place. On the dresser Layla spotted a photo of a younger Max and Ruby and picked it up.

"What the hell do you think you are doing?" screamed Kym, suddenly appearing in the doorway. "Get her out of here."

Startled, Layla ran through the back of the house, slipping on old magazines. Sometimes she thanked her rock climbing skills for helping her reflexes and balance.

Kym looked at Max with disdain. "How dare you bring someone else in here? What are *they* going to say? What are *people* going to say? You stay out of her room."

Max slammed his bedroom door and pushed his back against it, holding it shut. Kym banged on the door until she cried. Max stayed in his room for the rest of the night. His mind always ticking over. He would deal with her in the morning.

Max dreamt.

He walked through a large house with many corridors. The plaster on the old stonewalls had crumbled away. Timeworn floorboards lay bare; some had been pulled up, waiting for him to fall through. Eventually Max found his mother sitting in a chair in a large dark room.

"Come here," she said.

Max approached. Ruby stood before an open fire, her dress dirty and torn. Looking up, Max could see the clouds of a darkened sky through where the roof had rotted away and collapsed.

"Don't worry, Max," said Kym. "We have everything we need right here."

"Where's dad?" said Max.

Ruby pointed towards a door.

Max turned to see the flickering fire cast an orange glow over his father. A steering wheel dropped from his father's hand and rolled across the floorboards.

"Dad" said Max. "Are you coming in?"

Through the large bay windows at the end of the room, headlights exploded. The glare blinded them all. A car drove through the darkness, straight towards the windows as the house began to crumble and fall.

How many times? This same dream?

After a restless sleep, the dream retreated and the day invaded. Max, still in the clothes he fell asleep in, left through the window. His mother would not be awake, but he didn't dare risk crossing her. It was his final day of suspension and he wanted to enjoy it. He didn't want to spend the day around the house, feeling awkward in his own presence.

Max walked and skated. His only aim was to end up somewhere he didn't know, to lose himself in the city sprawl. Passing through the abandoned industrial buildings and the wetlands, Max crossed under a bridge that linked the two sides of the city. Once the sun began to lower in the sky, he turned around. Not knowing the way back home, he let his instincts guide him and just followed his feet. As the sun set, the air hung quiet and still, as if time had stopped.

Soon Max found himself in his suburb. Then at the end of his street. Then in front of his house.

Max took a deep breath and went inside.

Throwing his backpack on the bed, Max kicked a hole in the cupboard door. He was sick of it. Sick of the clutter. Sick of the mess. Sick of the useless junk his mother amassed. She walked the nearby streets, collecting whatever she could find. Someday, somehow, she would make something useful of all these things. Someday. Everything she found had value to her. Nothing could be thrown away, even though others had rightfully discarded it.

With a t-shirt tied around his face, Max entered the kitchen. Kym snored in front of the television. Emperor Norton slept curled up on her lap. Max began loading garbage into bags. He thought about how many times he had waited for dinner, only to find his mother passed out surrounded by a bottle or two. How many of those wine bottles still remained? Eventually, he gave up waiting. He learnt to feed himself, sometimes stealing money from his mother's purse. She would either not notice, or couldn't remember how much she had spent.

On the over grown nature strip, Max dumped the black rubbish bags. He had also moved an old hot water urn, three cracked mirrors and a broken LCD television. Stuffing a bag on top of the already full garbage bin, he hoped the garbage men would still collect it.

Max slumped down onto the grass. He felt hot and dirty and drained. He had moved six, maybe eight, bags of rubbish from the house. It was impossible to tell Max had made any attempt at cleaning. He could spend all night removing things and it would make no difference. Tomorrow the cleared spaces would be filled. Tomorrow. There would be more stuff tomorrow.

Looking at the stars, Max worried about what Layla would think of him now. She had witnessed the mess of his life, and the hoarder his mother had become. Max rolled over on the grass and let his gaze melt away. His eyes, bleary with exhaustion, focused on a piece of broken mirror. It angled at the recycling bin filled with newspapers. He noticed the symbol of the three arrows circling around the word 'recycle'.

15

In the quiet of morning, just before CrashCorp awoke, feet skipped lightly through the corridors, careful not to create a sound, or draw attention in any way. The humans would soon arrive, but for now there was a brief period where movement went unnoticed. Fingers pried the heavy steel door, inching it carefully open. An eye looked through the gap, spying the dummies asleep in their quarters, hanging from suspension hooks. Opening the door further, the figure slipped inside.

A dummy twitched while it slept, as spasm sparked in his shoulders and flickered through his fingers. "Noohaiidoohnntwhanntnacrahsh," he murmured.

Moving like stealth between the dummies the figure locked on what it was seeking.

A hand lashed out and grabbed a sleeping Hybrid's hand.

"Wake up," said a voice.

The dummy stirred all little.

"Mum. Wake up."

Feeling the tug on her hand, Astrid looked down to see Madison staring up at her.

"It's crash day," said Madison.

"Good morning little one," said Astrid.

"Let's go."

"Don't be so eager. We've got plenty of time. And we have to wait for the humans to turn up before we can crash."

"Crash?" The twitching dummies eyes sprung open. "Oh, no! What day is it? Today's today isn't it."

The dummy grappled at his suspension cable, fastened through the top of his head, and unclasped the hook.

"Quiet Sid," said Astrid. "You'll wake everyone."

"You're coming too," said Madison. She grabbed Sid's hand but he pulled it away.

"That certainly wasn't my decision. It would be polite if they asked first."

"You're being like a person," said Madison.

"'You're a Crash Test Dummy', they said. 'You will love it', they said. Really? Would I really? Just because I am a Crash Test Dummy, does that give them the right to put me in these so-called accidents?"

"Sid, relax," said Astrid. "If you don't put up such a fuss, it will make things easier for everyone. It will be a quick crash. Soon it will be all over. You'll be a step closer to Elcycer, and closer to seeing Sebastian again."

"You know, Astrid," said Sid, "you're right. Look at me carry on like I've never been sandwiched between two high speed vehicles before."

Sid patted himself down and regained his composure. Other dummies stirred awake.

"Is it too much for some quiet in the morning?" a Hybrid asked, rubbing its face.

"I'll just go for a walk to clear my head. I don't want to be a disturbance to anyone." Sid ducked out the door.

Sid and Sebastian had both started at the factory together, and while Sebastian had become the crash king, Sid's crash record had remained exceptionally low. Many wondered if he was ever likely to graduate, and he wondered the same thing.

Like all Crash Test Dummies, Sid had been looking forward to his first crash. The enthusiasm and encouragement from the new intakes of dummies had propelled Sid to believe he was about to have the ride of his life. He sat patiently, looking ahead, waiting for his car to start moving and the crash test to begin. Instead, he caught a glance of a four-wheel-drive hurtling towards him side-on.

Sebastian and the other Crash Test Dummies applauded from the sidelines. The unexpected side impact damaged more than his skeleton – his nerves were irreparably frayed. The crash never left his mind, replaying continuously. He also learnt one other thing, that he was unique to other dummies. Sid was a S.I.D, or a Side Impact Dummy, specifically designed to crash cars in the way his name suggested.

A human opened the door to the Hybrids' quarters, where the dummies were now awake.

"Astrid. Madison. Sid. You're up."

"It's time," said Madison, jumping up, pulling her mother along.

"Sid?" called the human, looking at them both.

Astrid gave an awkward smile.

The human folded his clipboard into his arms and let out a deep sigh. He slid the door closed across with a loud bang.

"He's gone missing again," called the human, as he entered the crash arena. The workers supervising the crashed looked at each other, not surprised by Sid's behaviour. "Send out a searched party for the rogue, and fit up a substitute. We need to get this show on the road. We've got a deadline, people."

The usual spaces were searched; storage cupboards, under stairwells, and in garbage bins. No luck. Sid had outsmarted the humans, which came as a relief to both parties. If found, it would have taken several humans to strap Sid into the car to prevent him from climbing out.

Astrid walked onto the crash test arena with Madison following just behind her. She was directed to the car and took her place in the driver's seat. Humans help strap Madison into the booster seat in the back. The vehicle was pushed into position.

A short siren blast filled the air as everyone cleared the crash floor. Lights flared up and the cameras begun recording.

Madison propped herself up, turned, and looked out the back window. She smiled as she saw another car race up from behind. It impacted with the trunk. Madison's head surged forward so that her face smashed on her knees. Her arms went limp, as they flew out, coming back to hit her. Her head slammed back into the seat.

The two cars had melded into one, the twisted metal intertwining and fusing together. Fragments tinkled to the crash floor.

Astrid turned to Madison, her shoulder twisted from the impact with the steering wheel.

"How was that?"

"Great," said Madison. Her neck was bent and she was unable to lift her head. She giggled.

Astrid gave a wave to the Crash Test Dummy in the car behind who had taken Sid's place. He waved, smiling through a dislocated jaw, and winking with his remaining good eye.

The humans approached and looked over the wreckage, pleased with their efforts.

Thumk. Thumk. Thumk.

The humans looked at each other, then back to the car. One took a few steps towards the wreckage and placed his head close to where the two cars had collided.

Thumk. Thumk.

"Get a crow bar over here now," yelled a human.

A worker came running across the crash floor. Together, they forced open the trunk of the front vehicle. It popped open with a screech.

"What is the matter with you people?" screamed Sid, sitting up inside the trunk. "What is this obsession with crashing? You people need help."

Sid tried to stand and step out of the trunk. He found his leg pinned in folds of metal.

"Oh, just fantastic," he cried. "What am I meant to do now? Walk around with a car as a shoe?"

"Someone cut this idiot out of my crash," said the supervisor, storming off the crash floor in a huff.

*   *   *

Astrid sat on a workbench as a technician used a drill to tighten up her shoulder. Madison lied on the workbench next to her mother as another technician worked on her neck. Sid sat on the chair, minus one leg, waiting his turn and thinking about what he had done.

"Congratulations Astrid," said the technician. "You've reached your target goal. You have completed enough crash tests to make your way to Elcycer."

"That's wonderful," she said. "When am I scheduled for graduation?"

"In just a few minutes."

"But, that isn't how things are done. Normally we—"

"Thing's have changed. Money is a bit tight and we've had to cut back on a few things," the technician lied. "We're streamlining our processes. Making them more efficient."

"Oh," said Astrid.

"You're all done."

Astrid tried moving her arm, but found her shoulder locked in place.

"This doesn't seem to be working!"

"Just a patch up for the moment. You'll get that finished off at Elcycer, we just don't have all the parts on hand."

"You're done too, Madison," said the other technician. She sat up and cricked her neck. "How is that?"

"Better."

"Now on to you, Sid. We can fix the physical problems, but it is the other kind of problems we can't fix."

"Just once I would like to see one of you humans in a crash test," said Sid. "We'll see how fond you are of crashing then."

"Okay, Astrid. It's time for you to go to Elcycer. I'll take you to the loading dock," said the technician.

Madison climbed down off the workbench, and Astrid knelt next to her.

"Madison, I have to go now. But, I will see you very soon."

"But, why?"

"I have to see your dad and Jupiter. They're waiting for us."

"Can I come?"

"Not yet. After a few more crashes. Stay with Sid, he'll look after you."

"We haven't got long," said the technician, "the truck is waiting."

Astrid gave Madison a hug with her good arm and kissed her on the forehead.

"Bye Madison."

"Bye mummy."

The technician walked Astrid to the door. He stood her against the wall, took a medal from his pocket and placed it around Astrid's neck. He took a photo and removed the medal.

Madison watched as the technician walked her mother away. She grabbed her broken doll and followed into the corridor. Sid hopped up on his remaining leg and hopped after them.

"Mummy."

Astrid turned.

"You didn't say good-bye to Beep Beep."

Astrid walked back and kissed the doll, then Madison again. Waving to Sid, she watched as he took Madison's hand, while doing his best to maintain his balance.

"I'll see you both at Elcycer soon."

16

As Max entered the school grounds he scanned for people's reactions. Everyone buzzed around in small swarms. A few kids snickered to each other as they passed by.

"I didn't think he'd be back."

"Ah, it's Max the Mower," some kid crowed.

The overwhelming response he had expected didn't eventuate. Everyone was happier dealing with the event by talking behind his back or making jokes, rather than challenging Max directly. This didn't upset him. It made things much easier. Everyone believed they knew what had occurred. They just needed to make a quick jab at Max throughout the day to remind him. This he could handle. It was better than facing a barrage of enquiring minds. He had a new plan. Keep a low profile for as long as possible and hope he fell off the schoolyard-talk radar.

Today Max and Layla's classes would not cross. He

spotted her a couple of times in the corridor, but only from a distance. Once they caught each other's glances, but Max looked away as though he was embarrassed. Max thought he would feel relieved he had let someone into his inner world, but he felt ashamed. None of his three therapists had ever ventured in so far. Max had turned up to the first couple appointments, only because he had to. He watched as they pretended they were his friends, and how they worked through the "tick the box" questions. They always looked bored and frustrated as they waited for a breakthrough. He gave them nothing. When he stopped turning up they would barely miss him. His appointment would be given to the next person willing to pay the hourly bill and Max's file would be destined for a cabinet where it would be forgotten.

First, whispers leapt between students, then beeps bounced between mobile phones. Collecting his books after lunch Max saw a bunch of students huddled around a phone as they watched a video. Another schoolyard fight? Another kid injured playing Wheelie Bin of Terror? A game where kids placed one of their mates in a wheelie bin and pushed them around until the willing victim could take no more.

Looking over a huddle of shoulders Max glimpsed something he recognised.

The grainy phone footage showed what appeared to be someone, a Crash Test Dummy, being struck by a bus. The bus tires screeched, sending up clouds of burnt rubber as the dummy flew into the air and crash-landed on the asphalt.

"Fake," someone cried.

"Na, it was on the news," another voice said. "It happened down at the mall."

Max watched himself and Layla run into the screen. He pulled Sebastian away from the bus, and they disappeared down the side of a shop.

"Who are the kids?"

"Probably someone from our school. The girl is wearing our sports uniform."

"Anyone know who it is?"

"It's too pixelated."

"Jemima Burstenstock reckons she does, but she's not allowed to tell."

"Oh, 'Miss I-Won-Three-Million-in-Lotto-but-I-Don't-Get-it-Until-My-Twenty-First-Birthday'? Yeah, right."

"First to track them down gets Jemima's millions." Others laughed as the second bell rang, signalling that everyone should be in class by now.

"Send it to me."

"Me too."

Max felt his stomach tighten. It would be only a matter of time before someone realised it was him in the footage. The crowd dispersed, disappearing down corridors and into classroom doorways.

Max felt dizzy. A hand touched him on the shoulder. He gave an almost catlike jump.

"Hey," said Layla. Max looked at her, stunned. "Have you seen the video?"

Max slowly nodded.

"Do you want to get out of here?" said Layla.

Max nodded his head again. He had watched his fair share of internet videos and knew how people loved being web sleuths. When Max was discovered, so was Sebastian.

"How about we go back to the treehouse?" said Layla.

"Na," said Max, "I need a little time to think. I've got another idea."

Max and Layla walked along the back streets, hoping not to be seen by anyone who would report them to the school. They crossed the train line and headed into the industrial estate. The concrete walls seemed bright as the sun burned over them.

"Is he safe?" asked Max.

"Still in the garden shed. I checked on him. Seems very determined to win hide-and-seek," said Layla. "Shouldn't be too hard to find out where Sebastian came from now. Someone's bound to see the video and want him back."

"I don't think it will be so easy as just handing him over," replied Max.

"We can't look after him forever," said Layla. "It's not like he understands how to keep himself inconspicuous. Besides, they can take him to Elcycer."

Max dropped to the ground, dumping his school bag beside him, and sat on the cracked footpath. Layla sat next to him. Max stared at his painting, glad it hadn't been painted over.

"That's pretty cool," said Layla. "Wish I could draw like that. I can barely manage a stick figure."

"I can," said Max. "And I did."

Layla glanced at Max, then back to the painting. Crumbling bricks edged the work, leaving the image of a gaping whole in the wall, bordering Max's graffiti. A scared alien hung desperately to the edge of the brickwork, fearful of being sucked into a black hole. The black hole drew everything towards it; planets, solar systems, a house, a crumpled car, and what looked like two souls. At first Layla thought it was cute, then began to examine it in more detail.

For a few minutes they sat in silence.

Cars rolled by.

"I feel like that alien," Max explained. "I don't remember too much about what happened. We were coming home from the movies, when headlights came out of nowhere. They didn't even try to stop. Just hit us. Ruby was in the back, right behind dad. I was in the passenger seat and tried to reach over to cover her. They just went straight into us. It sounded like the whole world was being ripped apart. I kept fading in-and-out of consciousness. I heard the footsteps of people running away." Max used his sleeve to wipe away tears. "They didn't even try to help us."

"Did they find who did it?" Layla asked.

"Stolen car," said Max. "They found half a bottle of whisky inside. I can't understand how you just destroy someone's life then pretend like nothing happened. She was only five. She never did anything to anyone. I was in a coma for two weeks, and when I woke up they were gone. I spent another month in hospital. I tried going back to school, but everyone just treated me like a freak. It wasn't like they were trying to do it. They didn't know how to react. I'd changed. They'd changed. Everything changed. I couldn't even get on the bus because I was afraid it would crash.

"Mum's been like a zombie ever since. She was working at the hospital as a triage nurse when the ambulance brought us in."

"Oh God," breathed Layla. She didn't know what else to say.

"Nothing's been the same," said Max. "One moment we were just living like normal people. Now she fills the house with rubbish to stop it feeling so empty. She had always collected stuff, but now there's so much mess that there's no way I can clean it up."

Max ran his hands down his face and pushed away the tears.

"I'm such a sook," he said.

"No." Layla placed her hands around Max's shoulders. "No, you're not."

"People kept telling me it would get better, but it doesn't."

"I'm sorry. I didn't know."

"We can't let them get Sebastian," blurted Max.

"You'll miss him too?" Layla asked.

"I know what Elcycer is."

Max pulled a textbook from his bag. He opened up the front cover. With a pen he wrote: *Elcycer*. Beneath it he wrote: *Recycle*.

"That's what they are going to do to him," said Max.

*　　　*　　　*

Lucinda stood on her penthouse balcony, as helicopters hovered like dragonflies against the rust coloured sunset sky. In the background the twenty-four-hour television news reports played.

She read a news article on her tablet. The article detailed Lucinda receiving an Environmental Invention Award at a brunch dedicated to her honour. She searched for where she had been quoted, checking to make sure they were word-perfect. They were.

"When I was struck with the idea for the advanced energy system for the EnviroCar, I went straight to the engineers, and asked, 'Is this possible?' At first we didn't know if it would work. I was told many times it was impossible, it couldn't be done. But, I was determined to see it to fruition and nothing was going to stop me."

She smiled.

The television diverted Lucinda's attention away from her script. She stepped inside, snatched the remote and turned up the volume to listen to the news report.

"Sketchy video footage has appeared on the internet of what appears to be a Crash Test Dummy involved in, what else, a traffic accident," read the news anchor. "The incident occurred at Redwood shopping mall. The footage has gone viral, with over a million views. It's unknown if the accident involved an actual Crash Test Dummy or it was an elaborate prank.

"Experts are already debating if a human could walk away from such and incident. Damage to the bus is expected to reach into the thousands. Authorities are concerned about the welfare of the individual involved and the teenagers witnessed running from the scene. Anyone with information should contact the police."

Muting the television, Lucinda dropped the remote and took hold of the phone. She auto-dialled a number.

The phone picked up. "Hello, CrashCorp."

"Get everyone organised," Lucinda said with a deathly dryness. "Now."

Within the hour, all the CrashCorp department heads had gathered around the boardroom table at headquarters.

"Everyone is on warning," said Lucinda, leaning on the table with her fists. "I'm not opposed to making anyone a sacrificial lamb. After watching the television reports, we are at code red. Sebastian must be found before the media finds him. We have a reputation to protect. CrashCorp's reputation will come before any individual. You all have your jobs to consider. Let's hear from around the table."

"I delivered a report two years ago. I suggested we track all Crash Test Dummies with GPS devices, just in case of such a situation. I was told this was unfeasible," said the head of dummy maintenance, sporting a comb over and potbelly.

"Well, you obviously didn't suggest hard enough," Lucinda responded.

"No Crash Test Dummy has survived more than a few

hours before crashing themselves," said the head of transportation. "They usually just run into traffic or find a car and crash into a wall. This is a rarity, even in global standards. We need to find who's looking after him."

"You finding another job will be a rarity if this isn't contained," said Lucinda. "It was your crew that lost him."

"That's right," said the head of security. "My records show he was sent to be recycled. Everyone involved in transportation needs to be questioned. Someone must be held accountable."

"Accountability. That is what is desperately lacking here," Lucinda said. "Some decisions are too hard to make, whether those decisions are made by an individual or a group. I'm sure you will all be thankful I'm not afraid to make the hard decisions. I have constructed a new team to counteract your mistakes."

Behind Lucinda mahogany doors opened. Two Thor Crash Test Dummies stepped forward. Another four Thors entered and assembled around the boardroom.

"Welcome to the next generation." Rising from her chair, Lucinda smiled. "You're safety is now in their hands. Thors will be taking a much more proactive role at CrashCorp. I'm sure you will make them most welcome."

17

"What are we going to tell him?" asked Layla.

"Nothing yet," said Max. "We have to find out everything he knows first. He might not realise he knows something that could lead us to Elcycer, or to where he's from."

Using the key handed to him by Layla, Max opened the timber door of the garden shed. A thick grey dust covered all the forgotten things. Max's hand reached out to an ancient oil-stained canvas tarpaulin. Pulling it away, he found Sebastian balled up in the corner, behind old wooden boxes.

Recognising the silhouette standing in the doorway against the sunset sky, Sebastian clambered to his feet. He leapt at Max, tackling him in an excited embrace. Max felt some of the wind leave him as he stumbled back and they both hit the ground. Sebastian almost resembled a dog seeing its owner after a long absence. Max gave a breathless laugh.

"Okay. Okay. Settle down Sebastian."

"I thought you hated me and I would never see you again. And I would have to spend every day with Layla. She's great, but you know . . . "

Layla gave a grunt of disapproval.

"How come you stay hidden when Max ask you to hide, but not when I do?"

"Max asks me to hide," said Sebastian.

"I've asked you to before," said Layla.

"You've never said 'hide'."

"Hide?" said Layla.

"Hide? Now?" said Sebastian.

"Take him up to the roof," she said. "I'll go find us something to eat and leave you guys to it."

Sebastian followed Max through the treehouse. He gazed around the city as the lights began switching on as the night crept in. In almost childlike wonder he became excited as bridges, streetlamps and signs of buildings lit up.

Layla's footsteps marched onto the deck. She carried two plastic bags.

"I've just found whatever I could raid from the cupboards and fridge. Cooking isn't a talent I'm blessed with."

"Me either," said Max.

Sitting on the rough wooden boards, Max and Layla began sorting through their bounty of chips, canned tuna, biscuits, pickled onions, mustard, bread rolls, salami and orange juice.

"It wouldn't hurt for my parents to buy a fresh vegetable once in a while. Everything else is packaged or frozen."

"Who cares? This is the best meal I've eaten in ages," Max said, stuffing his face with a bread roll filled with potato chips and a smothering of mustard.

"Should you let your mum know you won't be home for dinner?" asked Layla.

"I'm not going home tonight. It'll be okay. She won't even notice as long as I make an appearance in the next few days to remind her I'm still around."

Stretching out on the roof, Sebastian looked up to the sky. He saw lights moving against the deep blue of space and heard the delayed purring of engines.

"They have cars in the sky?" he said.

Surprised, Max coughed out some mustardy chips.

"It's a plane. They have wings and fly."

"What if it falls on us?"

"It won't. Well, hopefully not."

"Is it kept up by ropes?"

Max sighed. Being friends again with Sebastian made him feel better, but nevertheless it was still a frustrating task. Max crunched down on his roll.

"Someone's even turning on the stars." Sebastian's head darted around as he pointed from star to star. Every time he thought he had spotted them all, more appeared.

"Don't try counting them," said Layla. "There are trillions of them."

On the horizon Sebastian noticed one glowing brighter than all others.

"Look at how bright that star is," he said.

"It's not a star, it's a planet," said Layla. "That's Jupiter."

"Jupiter," whispered Sebastian.

"They used to be known as wandering stars." Layla finished off a can of tuna.

"Jupiter's my boy's name," said Sebastian.

Max and Layla looked up at each other over their food.

"You have a son?" Max said.

"The best little crasher I've ever come across. First in his class to graduate. It was a proud moment having him on stage with me. I can picture him now, running wild in Elcycer, tearing up the roads, levelling everything in his path."

"He left for Elcycer the same time you did?" Max swallowed hard on his food.

"Uh huh," Sebastian gave a proud nod.

"Oh no. We have to find Elcycer." Layla reached for her laptop and flipped open the screen. Max came around and helped her search. Sebastian fascinated himself with the stars and watched aeroplanes skim across the sky.

They tried various queries in the search engine. Half an hour passed with no luck. Most searches didn't bring up any useful results. They tried looking for car manufacturers in the area. An advertisement appeared in the results.

"Why do I know that logo?" Layla wondered aloud.

"My dad used to work there for a while," said Max.

"No, that's not—" Layla paused. "Sorry?"

"That logo is on a mug my dad gave me. He worked there. He used to make me hot chocolate in it."

"What did he do there?" asked Layla.

"Don't know. It was just where he worked. He started working at CrashCorp just before the . . ."

"Did he ever say if they had dummies there?"

Max shook his head. "He never talked about his work at all. It was just a place where he went in the morning and came home from at night."

Max thought for a moment and pulled out his phone. He flicked through his collection of photos and found one of his father trying to ride Max's skateboard. Max had laughed when he fell off, but looking back at the photo the memory didn't even bring a smile.

"Do you recognise him?" Max said, holding the phone in front of Sebastian.

"Dan, the toy man?" smiled Sebastian.

"What?" said Max.

"He brought the children toys. I haven't seen him around for ages."

"You wouldn't," said Max.

Layla turned her laptop around and pointed at the logo on the screen.

"Have you seen this before?"

"The factory insignia."

"So he's from CrashCorp," said Layla.

Layla clicked on the link and opened the CrashCorp website. The logo flashed onto the screen in a series of animated effects. A streamlined car drove in, parked itself in the centre of the screen, and began rotating three-hundred-and-sixty degrees. Underneath, the words *The Future is Here* faded in.

"That's where I've seen it before. It's been all over the news," said Layla.

"It's the car I did my most spectacular crashes in. You should see the damage I did to that baby," said Sebastian.

Clicking on the rotating car a video appeared on screen.

"Welcome to CrashCorp. World leaders in car automotive design, manufacturing and safety.

"CrashCorp is proud to introduce the world's first fully functional electric car. With patented technology and unique paint formulation, the EnviroCar uses solar energy absorbed directly through the exterior paint, and stores the energy in a custom designed fuel cell. The EnviroCar automatically recharges, never requiring an additional fuel source.

"Using patented technology, the EnviroCar is the most advanced environmental and consumer friendly car the world has ever known. With the EnviroCar, everyone can breathe a clean sigh of relief, knowing The Future is Here."

"Did I do good?" Sebastian asked.

"You did," said Max. "Tell us again what happened when you graduated."

Sebastian told them about the stage and the lights and the medals and the photograph. How they all rode in the back of a truck to Elcycer, until he fell out. Sebastian didn't know where he had fallen. It was his first introduction into this strange land. He only remembered being surrounded by lights that alternated between green and red.

Max looked up a map, and pinned a placemark at CrashCorp, located on the other side of the city. He stuck another placemark where he had done his graffiti and first met Sebastian. There were several intersections with traffic lights surrounding that spot, a few with main roads crossing them. Sebastian could have fallen out at any of them.

Layla leaned over and whispered to Max. "Search for car recycling yards."

"There are even more stars now," said Sebastian. "I'm going to catch one and keep it as a pet."

Max searched. Several recycling yards popped up around the city outskirts. He followed the path from CrashCorp to where he had found Sebastian. Continuing on he traced with his finger on the screen until it led him to a recycling yard buried deep in the outer suburbs.

"I think I've found something," said Max.

18

"I guess it won't hurt if he falls out," said Max.

Barely fitting inside a small red wagon salvaged from Max's garage, Sebastian sat with his knees tucked up to his chest. Layla had fashioned a towrope from abseiling gear and hitched the wagon to their bikes. With no brakes on the wagon, she demonstrated to Sebastian how to stop by pressing his hands on the road; they would give him the signal when to do so.

The scrap yard was located several kilometres away. They took the familiar back streets to avoid being confronted by the invasive headlights of passing cars. Making their way down a suburban street, they came to a dead end. Sebastian dragged his hands along the asphalt, until his wagon came to a stop.

Hiding their bikes in bushes, the trio slid their way along a small embankment leading down to a storm catchment channel running along the back of the scrap yard. The channel was mostly dry. Barely a trickle ran along the open expanse. Discarded shopping trolleys, having spent their last moments as speed racers, lay upturned among the debris of plastic bottles and branches.

Under the cover of trees lining the fence, Max pulled a pair of pliers from his pocket. He begun cutting through the chain link fencing. They had ridden passed the front of the scrap yard, seeing a middle aged man sitting in the guard box. He didn't notice them as they steadily moved passed on the far side of the road. He didn't even look up from his puzzle.

Cutting through the last link, the fence sprung back, revealing an opening. A wirily ping echoed along the fence, reverberating through the night air. Looking at each other, they waited for any indication that they had been detected.

"Welcome to Elcycer," said Max.

Max went through the fence first. Taking Sebastian's hand, he led him through, followed by Layla. Old car bodies were parked in rows, their final resting place. Some had been stripped of parts. The air held an eerie quiet.

"It feels like we're in a graveyard," said Max.

"In some way we are," said Layla.

"This isn't what I thought Elcycer would look like at all," said Sebastian. "It is, but it's not. These cars are already crashed. And where is everyone? The heroes who came before?"

"That's what we have to find out," said Max, pulling a printout of a satellite image from his shorts pocket. Each crunch of gravel under their feet sounded as though it was sending out an alarm.

"Sebastian is there anything you recognise?" asked Layla.

Sebastian scanned the area. He recognised car bodies, but none he had been responsible for crashing. They were once useful, but now they were just twisted shells. In the dim lights they appeared to cry out for a second chance.

"That! I've seen that at the factory." Sebastian pointed to a solid metal gate, brown with rust. A sign with a company logo read: Property of CrashCorp – Unauthorised Access Prohibited.

Max scanned the map. A sectioned off corner of the scrap yard housed more car bodies and two shipping containers. They ran over to the gate and peered through a gap.

"That's the EnviroCar," said Layla.

"Or what's left of it," said Max.

"My pride. That's the car that made me the hero you see before you today," said Sebastian, wearing his torn overalls and dirt covering the side of his face.

Layla stepped back and assessed the fence. Dumping her backpack on the ground, she pulled out a rope and carabiners. Tying the rope around Sebastian, Layla fashioned a makeshift harness. With a forceful heave, she threw the other end over the gate.

"I'll go over first. You follow," Layla instructed to Max.

With ease, Layla scaled the fence, securing her footing on rivets to boost herself up. From the top of the fence, she could see over the yard, all the way to the guard box. Max's attempt was much more awkward. Laying flat along the steel girder, Layla reached down and clasped Max's hand. With a firm pull, Max was able to scramble his way up.

"Getting down is going to be the easy bit," Layla said. "Now for the tricky part. Sebastian, try to get over as best you can. We'll pull you up from the other side."

Layla and Max dropped to the ground. Layla fastened two carabiners to car bodies forming a pulley system. Handing the rope to Max, she stood behind him.

"Pull."

Sebastian jolted forward. The sound of Sebastian crashing against the gate bounced around the yard, drawing the security guards attention. With their feet slipping on the gravel, Max and Layla pulled the taut rope. Their efforts were much louder than expected. Sebastian slid up the gate. His arm appeared over the top.

"Keep going," Max strained.

In a mix of twisted limbs, Sebastian came crashing over the gate, landing face first on the ground.

"Touchdown," boomed Sebastian.

With his feet skidding in the dirt, Max ran over to Sebastian. Jumping on top of him, he clasped his hand over Sebastian's mouth. Peering through the gap between the gate and the fence, Max eyed the guard. Torchlight swung between the mangled car bodies, reflecting off broken windscreens.

"Don't move," whispered Max.

The guard passed in front of the gate. The flashlight

darted through the gap. He paused. The beam of light sliced through the crack, barely missing the pair. The guard headed back, inspecting cars as he left. A cry sounded as the security guard walked into a length of metal hanging off a crippled courier van. He rubbed his eye. Swearing, he struck the metal with his torch. Wiping a trace of blood from his face he stormed back to the guard box.

"It's clear." Max signalled to Layla who hid behind a pile of parts.

Sebastian stood up and looked around in amazement. "These crashes have been my most spectacular moments." He raced over to a mangled wreck of a red vehicle. "You should have seen this one. My best pal Sid, catapulted through the window with such force, they were putting him back together for weeks. And this one here, Madison was the hero of this crash. Six attempts it took them to get the air bags working." Sebastian turned to Max, "Aren't crashes just great?"

Max stood looking over the graveyard of cars. He couldn't engage in Sebastian's excitement.

"What's the matter little human?" asked Sebastian, placing his hand hard on Max's shoulder, breaking his trance.

"Nothing," said Max. "I'm fine."

"Thanks for bringing me here. Soon we will find everyone else in Elcycer. Bet they're sleeping."

"Over here," Layla called from in front of a shipping container.

The shipping container door squealed open. Layla took two LED headlamps from her bag and handed one to Max. The lights lit up the inside of the container. The body parts of Crash Test Dummies lined the walls. Arms, legs, torsos, and complex internal mechanics were divided up into groups. Wooden crates piled up, with labels stating their contents. A partly deconstructed Crash Test Dummy lay on a workbench.

"Oh wow," said Layla. "This is unreal." Stepping into the container she picked up a forearm with a hand attached.

"Hi, guys." She waved the arm at Max and Sebastian.

Seeing the blank looks on their faces, she placed the arm down.

Sebastian stepped passed her. He slowly ran his hand over different dummy parts.

"I'm sorry," whispered Layla.

Placing a finger to his lips, Max gestured for her to say nothing. Max stood at the door, lighting the way for Sebastian. He moved along the wall. His mechanical heart sunk with every moment.

Max pulled out his phone and took photos as he followed Sebastian. The flash lit up the interior of the container. Layla looked at him, unsure if he was being disrespectful.

"We might need it as evidence," said Max. Layla also took out her phone.

Finding a cracked breastplate, he unhooked it from the wall. Sebastian looked at the partly deconstructed dummy on the bench. It had been degloved, revealing its skeleton, and all the circuitry had been removed.

"Astrid," mouthed Sebastian. He turned and looked at Max and Layla. "What have you humans done? She was my wife." He dropped the breastplate to the floor.

"Demolition Doug." Sebastian picked up a latex face. "He was my mentor."

Searching the tangled mess of parts, he found a small faceplate near a pair of tiny folded overalls.

"Hey, Jupiter."

"We didn't know if it was true," said Max. "Elcycer is 'recycle' spelt backwards. We were hoping they would be okay."

"We thought we could liberate them, or something," added Layla.

Sebastian held up Jupiter's metal skull. "You have to put him back together. You have to put them all back together. I've seen it done before."

Layla looked to Max.

"We can't," Max said, swallowing his words. "They're gone."

"But they're *here*," said Sebastian.

Max walked up to Sebastian. "We can't do anything. We have to go."

Holding Sebastian's arms they led him from the shipping container. Layla pushed the door closed and locked it. Max walked Sebastian over to piles of car bodies stacked against the outside fence. He became slow on his feet. Climbing up the cars, they peered over the fence. Max swung himself down, landing in the overgrown grass.

Sebastian turned and stared over the scrap yard.

"This is Elcycer? They threw us away," he said solemnly. "But, we're meant to be heroes."

Layla joined Sebastian. "We can't stay here. It's not safe."

"But what about . . ." started Sebastian.

The bouncing flashlight flickered through the darkness as the security guard ran towards them. Thieves regularly jumped over the fence to steal parts. It was easier to chase them away than go through the effort of making a report. If they made any significant damage, he could hide it for someone else to discover later.

He shone the flashlight up to see the figures against the back fence.

Kicking as hard as she could, Layla connected with Sebastian's hip. He fell over the fence and to the ground. Hitting the embankment he rolled into the storm water channel. Max slid down the embankment, finding Sebastian stunned and looking towards the stars.

"Are you okay?" Max asked.

Sebastian's eyes turned slowly towards him.

It took more than an hour to get home. Even though their tow system had been the same, dragging Sebastian along seemed much harder. Max and Layla had grown tired. Sebastian slumped in the wagon, becoming a dead weight. Slipping the bikes into low gear proved hard work. Rolling down the alley, they approached the back of Layla's house.

"We're going to stop, Sebastian," called Max. They

pressed on the brakes.

Sebastian's hands failed to go down. He sat there like a dummy. The wagon trundled between their bikes and the ropes pulled them forward. Awkwardly Max leapt from his bike. Layla tried to do the same, but the frayed leg of her pants caught on the seat, yanking her, the bikes, Sebastian, and the wagon into a large twisted mess.

It was the first crash Sebastian had not enjoyed. He remained motionless in the entanglement, with the bluestone pavers pressed against his face.

Max and Layla untied the bikes. As though they were moving a body, they dragged Sebastian to the treehouse.

"Do you think we short-circuited him?" asked Max.

"I'm going to get some coffee. It's going to be a long night," said Layla, heading towards the house.

Max carefully led Sebastian up the stairs, onto the roof, and sat him against the railing. For a long while they sat looking over the city. Airplanes and police helicopters hovered silently against the stars.

"Are you okay?" asked Max.

Sebastian's face looked full of sadness. A face that longed for tear ducts.

"It hurts."

19

DANGEROUS DUMMY DISASTER

Police have confirmed a Crash Test Dummy has escaped from the CrashCorp automotive facility.

The escape comes as CrashCorp celebrates the record sale figures for the EnviroCar.

The Dummy is considered dangerous and could be armed. It should not be approached under any circumstances.

Lucinda Craven, CrashCorp CEO, released a statement earlier today.

"This is a very unfortunate incident. CrashCorp staff are doing their best to contain the situation. This is a one off occurrence. We have never had such a security breach before."

A $10,000 reward has been offered by CrashCorp for

information leading to the capture of the Crash Test Dummy.

The dummy escaped while being transported to a cleaning facility.

A video, which went viral, captured the moment the dummy was struck by a bus at Redwood Mall. The video, which has received almost 2 million views, shows two youths fleeing with the dummy.

Paramedics attended to the bus driver, Louis Hoy, after the incident.

"I thought I'd killed someone. Then they ran off. I've barely been able to sleep since. Forty-five years I've been driving and I've never seen anything like it."

Damage to the bus is estimated at $6,000.

Anyone with knowledge of the whereabouts of the Crash Test Dummy should contact their local police station.

It is alleged the dummy broke into a Westville business overnight, where a security guard was injured, sustaining a black eye.

"It's a police matter. I can't talk about it," said security guard Keith Cunard.

It is not known if anything was stolen from the business or the reason behind the break in.

A press conference is scheduled for later today.

*   *   *

Fixing her make-up in the bathroom, Lucinda checked herself over as she spoke to her assistant.

"I can't believe it," beamed Lucinda. "I couldn't give a rats about that stupid dummy, but frankly his going missing is the best thing that could have happened. Look at all this publicity. You would have to kill someone to get this much media attention. I actually thought he would have crashed himself into splinters by now."

"Remember," said her assistant, "no matter what questions they ask, bring everything back around to your book."

"Sweetness. Darling," Lucinda turned, "I've been working things in my favour long before you were even thought of. Hand me my purse, then go and check outside. I have to know what to expect."

Her assistant took a quick look around the foyer.

"Lights. Cameras. The place is packed to the door. Play this right, and we could go global."

"Time to milk the cow."

Lucinda pushed the door open. She stepped up to the rostrum to meet with several camera flashes. Her stern face held as she let the audience settle down. Her icy blue eyes ran their gaze over everyone in the crowd. Tipping her glasses to the end of her nose, she looked down to her speech.

"This morning we were confronted with distressing news that there had been a breach of security at CrashCorp, something quite serious. This matter has distressed everyone at CrashCorp and all whom have worked hard on the EnviroCar. One of our members was injured last night during a break in at one of our cleaning facilities. Our thoughts are with him.

"The EnviroCar has been a life long ambition of mine to help all of humanity. What better way to do this than ensure a lasting environmentally sound means of transportation?

"To harbour a safe future, we must harbour a safe environment. I have always believed the welfare of others is paramount. In my autobiography, *Time to Ride*, I illustrate my humanitarian ambitions . . ."

*   *   *

Max and Layla watched the webcast from the treehouse. The footage of the bus incident played in the corner of the screen, followed by a number to call to report information.

Sebastian had resigned himself to the hammock on the deck, staring at the sky for hours.

Max had been researching what happens to Crash Test Dummies after they had been dismantled. What he found wasn't very positive. He came across the news articles about Sebastian. They had not expected their visit to the recycling yard to receive so much attention.

"That guard wasn't injured because of us!" said Layla.

"I don't think anyone is going to believe us," said Max. "We did break in. And they got their side of the story out first. We're involved in something much bigger than we thought."

"We can't hand Sebastian over," said Layla. "They'll have him in parts in no time, just to protect their image. No one knows it was us. The video footage is so pixelated."

"I don't think it will be long now until someone figures it out," said Max. "We're going to have to find somewhere to hide Sebastian."

*   *   *

Layla's mother ran her finger around the edge of the white marble bench top, checking for any invisible imperfections. Gazing out into the backyard, she pictured where the conservatory would go. The building refuse vanished to reveal an antique wrought iron dining table, under a glass ceiling. Wisterias dropped purple flowers as the winter retreated and spring marched on. In summer it would form a thick canopy of vines.

A sale date for the house had been scheduled, and a consultation with the real estate agent marked in her diary. The landscape of the garden she wished for unfolded in her mind. After the old shed and laundry were demolished, the builders would clean out the rubble and the bobcat would need to be called in. The ground had already been checked for pipes. The eyesore of the treehouse could finally be dismantled. The trees cut down and the roots excavated.

A knock came from the restored oak front door. She imagined the sound of a cast iron knocker or video intercom buzzer instead. As she stepped across the floor, her high heels sounded like hammers on the boards.

Opened plaster bags, toolboxes and left over skirting board lined the passage.

She opened the door with a warm smile, imagining outside was an English cottage garden. Two police officers stood on the porch. Her smile vanished.

"Are you the guardian of Layla Ramos?" asked Senior Constable Billing.

Her mouth instantly went dry and she felt her stomach sink.

"I think you better come in," she said.

In what would one day be the formal lounge room, they sat on couches covered with drop sheets.

"Would you like tea?" A nervous tone wavered in her voice.

"We're fine."

"What's this about?"

"I would like to show you some video footage." Constable Grieves pulled out a tablet and played the video.

Mrs Ramos covered her mouth as she watched. Even through the pixelated image, she instantly recognised Layla's shape. Her heart pounded.

"Is that Layla?" asked Constable Grieves.

"This doesn't make sense. Layla would never be involved in such things."

"Do you know anything about a Crash Test Dummy?"

"Excuse me?"

"Do you recognise the young male in the video?"

"I didn't even know Layla had any friends. We haven't lived here very long." For the first time, Layla's mother realised how little she knew about her own daughter.

"Do you know where Layla is?" asked Billing.

"She's most likely in her—" She paused, feeling embarrassed that her daughter was living in a treehouse. "I will just go get her."

"Could you take us to her, please?" asked Grieves.

Her embarrassment was soon overtaken by a sense of dread. Could Layla be associated with a Crash Test Dummy escapee? A barrage of images invaded her mind. The Department of Human Services would be called in. She would have to explain why her daughter was living in a treehouse. The council would inspect the property. Fines would be issued for establishing a structure without a permit. Court might follow. Newspapers would pick up the story. She would be painted as a horrible mother who abandoned her child and forced Layla to live outside. This could slow down the renovation by months, or even put it on hold permanently. None of this is what she had planned.

She led them to the backyard and motioned towards the treehouse.

"Does she spend much time in there?" Billing enforced an air of seriousness. He asked further questions about Layla's living conditions while Constable Grieves pulled down the ladder and climbed inside the treehouse.

"Wish I had a place like this when I was a kid," she said to herself. At least this callout was a break from the constant calls to assist with the perpetual fights and burglaries they usually attended. On the tree trunk

Constable Grieves noticed something.

She descended the ladder.

"I think you should have a look at this," said Grieves, holding up the crash symbol sticker from Sebastian's head; a circle divided into quarters, coloured black and yellow.

"Do you know what this is, Mrs Ramos?" asked Billing.

"Oh dear," she said, pinching her forehead. In her mind, the perfect image of her house imploded, leaving only a giant cloud of dust.

20

Climbing to the top of the grassy hill, Sebastian, Max and Layla looked over CrashCorp. Floodlights escaped through the cyclone fencing. Air hung heavily with humidity. The last of the orange sunset vanished. The factory appeared as though it had just begun to slumber. Birds gave their last chirps goodnight before settling in. The hum of traffic resonated throughout the city. Layla rifled through her bag, searching for the right abseiling gear.

Sebastian sat beside Max, lost in a fixed stare. Max worried that Sebastian may remain this way forever. Getting him to the grounds outside CrashCorp had not been difficult. Sebastian had become easy to control. Just a matter of leading the way and he did as instructed, much like controlling a mindless robot. Sebastian had finally become no trouble, but Max wasn't sure if he liked it. He *knew* he didn't like it.

"If they're going to come looking for us, the last place they're going to search is where they expect us to stay away from," said Max.

"I've never seen it from this side before," said Sebastian.

"Hey. You're talking again."

Layla's phone rang. The caller ID flashed *MUM*. She nervously answered.

"Hello."

"Hi, Poppy. Are you okay? Where are you?"

Layla hung up.

"She knows. She called me Poppy. She hasn't called me that since pageants."

"Poppy?" glowed Max.

"Shut up or I will start breaking bones."

"How much do you think she knows?"

Layla brought up the local newspaper on her phone. Sebastian's image appeared on the front page under breaking news.

"I told you I'm famous," said Sebastian.

Clicking on the link, a video began to play. The female news presenter spoke to the camera.

"Fears are held tonight for two teenagers. Max Alderson and Layla Ramos have been reported missing by police. It is possible an escaped Crash Test Dummy may have abducted the pair."

"Abducted?" said Max.

"I am really, really famous," said Sebastian, looking at his CrashCorp mug shot on screen.

"This is not the kind of famous you want," said Max.

"A Crash Test Dummy, known as Sebastian, is considered unstable, and should not be approached under any circumstances."

"No need for insults," gasped Sebastian. "Just because I'm not human doesn't mean I don't have feelings."

"It's just the news," said Max. "That's what they do."

"How come the news is different from what is really happening?" asked Sebastian.

"They make things more entertaining so people will watch it," said Layla. She turned off the video.

"We have to decide if we're really going to do this," she said.

"What if we go in and I get stuck back in there forever?" said Sebastian. "I used to think the whole world was inside the factory. But the world is bigger than I ever imagined. It goes all the way to the bridge. I don't want to live back in the factory. I want to see the stars."

"We're not going to stay there," said Max. "We're just gonna break the other dummies out, so they can also see the stars."

"I don't know if I can. I don't want to end up in pieces."

The phone rang again. Max and Sebastian watched as Layla answered. She listened to the caller.

"Okay," she responded in a soft voice.

With the caller still speaking, Layla hung up.

"The police. They want us to come home. They said they don't want this to get to a level where they'll have to use force against Sebastian."

"What did I do?" Sebastian pressed his hand to his

chest.

"So we go home," said Max. "And then what? They recycle him. We just pretend nothing happened. I'm sorry, but I really don't want to deal with the police at the moment. I'm in enough trouble as it is. If I have to talk to them, I'd rather do something to grab their attention. Besides, the police can't help us. They couldn't find who caused my accident. The last place the police will look for us is in there."

Layla's phone rang again. She turned it off.

"You might want to shut off your phone in case they try to track it."

Max took out his phone and turned it off.

"If we do this, there is no going back," said Layla.

"If we return now, it will be over," said Max. "Either way, we'll still be in trouble. If we don't stand up for ourselves no one else is going to."

"We must free everyone," said Sebastian with regained confidence. "Show them what it's like on the outside. I know the factory. I know every inch of the place." Sebastian looked at Max and Layla with a determined glare. "Welcome to my world."

*　　*　　*

Pushing the pliers into his pocket, Max held open the fence as Sebastian and Layla crawled through. The trio darted up the side of CrashCorp.

Peering around the corner, Sebastian pointed. "There it

is."

"Stay here," said Max, before creeping along the wall to a roller door. Reaching up from behind the loading platform, Max pressed the button to raise the door.

The door failed to lift. Locked.

Max glanced back at Sebastian and Layla. He shook his head.

Click.

The side door opened and a worker stepped out onto the platform.

Max hit the ground. The pounding of his heart and the rush of blood filled his whole body. Holding as still as the night air, he even tried to keep his breathing to a minimum.

Max heard a rasping of metal. Moments later cigarette smoke wafted down to him. Max could hear the worker pacing above his head. Small stones and dust skipped across the platform, pushed by the workers boots, and rained into Max's hair.

Minutes crawled by.

How long does it take to smoke a cigarette? Max wondered.

He heard the sound of the sensor beep as the worker swiped his security pass. The door hissed open. He peeked over the platform to see the back of the worker disappear into the factory.

Pulling the pliers from his pocket, Max slid them across the platform. Holding his breath, he watched the pliers hit the doorframe. The door automatically pulled shut, wedging the pliers, leaving the door ajar.

Max watched for several seconds to make sure the worker had not noticed. He waved for the others to join him. Creeping along the wall, they pulled themselves up onto the platform and entered CrashCorp.

Sebastian led Max and Layla through the maze of corridors, the same he had last walked along when graduating from CrashCorp. The factory seemed quieter than usual, even for nighttime. It wasn't as Sebastian remembered. The factory he had known as a place where dreams existed had been transformed into a place of destruction. A place where dummies lived a lie, unsuspecting of the reality awaiting them outside.

Along the corridor walls, before the doors entering onto the crash arena, graduation photographs hung of all the dummies who had reached the status of hero. The history of all the dummies who had lived their lives at CrashCorp was on display. The Honour Wall. Sebastian could find no honour in how they had been treated.

"None of them ever got their medals back," said Sebastian. "It was another empty promise."

"I never thought there would be so many," said Max, as he closely examined the photographs. Some dated back to long before his birth.

"There you are Sebastian," said Layla. "More have graduated since you."

Sebastian looked at the recent photos. He pointed at one.

"Astrid," whispered Sebastian.

Sebastian's eyes darted over the photos. Every dummy gave a proud smile, holding up their medals. Some sat their children on their shoulders.

"She's not there," said Sebastian.

"Who isn't?" asked Max.

"Madison." Sebastian smiled at Max and Layla. "My daughter. She must still be here."

"You also have a daughter?" said Max.

Aware of how heavy every footstep sounded, Sebastian led Max and Layla along corridor after corridor. He pushed open the door to the quarters where the dummies slept. The spaces where his companions once hung were now empty, except for one. They slowly moved through the room.

Sebastian scanned the empty places, reading the name signs. Dummies once filled every spot. They would high-five each other as they returned from crash tests. Tales of heroic crashes sounded throughout the night, told and repeated. And repeated. Advice on crash techniques were shared and demonstrated. Together they dreamed of when it would be their turn to walk through the gates of Elcycer.

Approaching the lone dummy, Sebastian carefully placed a hand around the back of the dummy's head and clasped his other hand over his mouth.

The dummy's eyes shot open. His limbs flayed as he kicked about in an uncoordinated panic.

"Shhh. Sid, it's Sebastian."

It took Sid a couple of seconds to recognise his old friend. He blinked as he processed what was going on.

Sid stopped panicking and Sebastian removed his hand.

"Sebastian?"

"We're going to get you all out of here."

"Oh, thank heavens," said Sid. "I don't know if my nerves could take another crash."

Sebastian unhooked Sid from his support.

"Why aren't you at Elcycer?"

"There are many, many questions in the Universe, but so very, very few answers," said Sebastian in a moment of profoundness in that he wasn't quite sure he'd had.

21

Leading Sid from the sleeping quarters, Sebastian eased the door closed. The four of them stood in the corridor. Sebastian looked around, staying alert for any humans. The cool night air contracted the steel frames of the factory, causing the building to clang and drone.

"Where is everyone else?" Sebastian asked. "Have they all graduated?"

"Not everyone," said Sid. "They're holding graduations all the time. Another is happening now. They've really cut back on the flair. You just get your medal and you're on the truck to Elcycer. I've been banned from attending this one because I 'didn't comply to company standards.' I think they're trying to make an example of me."

"Is Madison graduating?" Sebastian asked.

"I don't think so," said Sid. "Madison hasn't been the same since Astrid graduated. She keeps walking around looking for her mum. Sometimes at night we can hear her screaming because of nightmares. She just wants to go to Elcycer so she can be with her mother.

"She's even had fights with the humans. She's been refusing to crash. She bit a human as they tried to strap her into a car. Got him a good one. 'Stop behaving like Sid,' they said. Blatant disrespect and they still expect me to crash. They can forget it." Sid's voice had grown louder.

Sebastian clasped his hand over Sid's mouth again. "We can't let the humans know we're here."

"I don't know if I can take anymore of this. Let's just skip all the crashing and go straight to Elcycer."

"We can't," said Sebastian.

"You know where it is, take me there. Just let me be happy like everyone else," pleaded Sid.

"Elcycer's not what you think," said Sebastian.

"Never is. It's always better," said Sid. "Otherwise everyone would come back."

"There is no Elcycer. There's no Land of Heroes," explained Sebastian.

"Don't be ridiculous, of course there is. It is a land full of everything a dummy could want. Where we meet our forefathers. Dummies are free to live how they please. You don't even have to crash if you don't want to."

"Sid," said Sebastian. "Elcycer is a lie. It's a recycling station."

"That's a lie," Sid fired back.

"Show him on the oracle," Sebastian said to Max.

Max powered up his phone and flicked through the

photos from the recycling station. He pulled up a photo of the body parts hanging on the wall. He showed them to Sid, sliding his finger over the screen to reveal each photograph. Sid leant in to see. His face took on a look of horror.

"Humans did this?" Sid asked. Stepping back against the wall, he pointed at Layla and Max. "Why did you bring them here? They just want to destroy us all."

"We don't," said Layla. "We want to help you. We want to get you out of here."

"You want me to trust you? You take us away. Then take us apart."

Pushing his hands against Sid's shoulders, Sebastian pinned him against the wall.

"Calm down. They didn't know. There are lots of humans outside the factory. All different. More twisted and bizarre than you could imagine. Each one freakier than the next."

Max and Layla glanced at each other, both taking offence.

"It's just the humans in the factory who want to do that to us," continued Sebastian.

"They can do what they like. We're indestructible." Sid paused and thought about what he had just said. He weighed this up against the photos he had seen. "Oh."

"Yeah, oh," said Sebastian. "We have to find Madison and get you guys out of here."

"We are heroes, not spare parts. Talk about ungrateful. I need a lie down," Sid said.

"Why do you think we're here? We've come to help you escape," said Max.

"We've been hiding Sebastian to make sure no one from CrashCorp finds him. We can help you too," said Layla, unsure if that was true.

"It doesn't seem like there is much left for us now, considering *they* have taken over," said Sid.

"Who's taken over?" Sebastian asked.

"Thors," stuttered Sid. "The new Crash Test Dummies started coming the night you graduated. That's just the beginning. We heard the truck roll up outside and when the doors open, they marched passed us in straight rows. Everyone was in awe. They looked so beautiful and clean and strong. I didn't like their attitude, but if they're willing to do the crashes, fine by me."

Max and Layla were both amazed by how fast Sid could talk.

"Graduations went into high gear. Dummies were shipped off all the time. Some hadn't even finished their crash quota. Before we knew it, Thors had taken over. Us Hybrids were shoved aside. And they're not very nice. They separated families. Children graduated without their parents knowing. It was never like this with you around. I don't like it at all."

"And there are more leaving tonight?" asked Max.

"I won't be. I'm afraid I might be stuck here forever," said Sid. "Can you imagine? With those brutes around? My life will be even more torturous. Can't even dream that someone would come along and rescue me."

"That's what we're here for," said Layla.

"Well, I thought you would be a little taller. Have you met a Thor?" asked Sid. "Bossy, very bossy. The kids don't like them. But, there are only a few kids left now."

Sebastian placed a hand on each side of Sid's face. "Sid, you have to focus. Where is Madison?"

"They banned her from the graduation for biting that human. If anything, she should be up there getting a medal."

"Sid," blasted Sebastian.

"I think she's locked in the children's quarters until she complies," said Sid.

"Follow me," said Sebastian.

He led everyone through the corridors until they reached the children's sleeping quarters.

Clutching the handle of the heavy steel door, Sebastian heaved it open.

22

Thors marched onto the crash test floor with military precision, forming one line behind the other. Their yellow shells, which covered their replicated human skeletons, glinted under the spotlights. Each Thor was new, unmarked and unscathed. All looked forward to their first crash, but there was one thing in their way – Hybrids.

Even without any crash experience, all Thors prided themselves with a certain smugness, confident their crash test abilities far excelled that of the Hybrids. It was an untested truth at CrashCorp. Thors were a technological advancement in Crash Test Dummy evolution, decades of development provided Thors with more humanlike qualities. Electronic sensors had been integrated throughout their bodies, able to detect high degrees of sensitivity not possible with the Hybrids. Thors not only detected the breaking of limbs, but also muscle damage, bruising, nerve damage, and internal injuries.

A brand new face had been designed for the Thors, able to extract data from facial trauma. Their unique bodies displayed not only the development of Crash Test Dummies, but also a new level of human technological sophistication. The improvements of the spine and pelvis made Thors more humanlike then ever. In some ways they were more human than they recognised.

The glass doors on the observation deck hissed open. Lucinda stepped out onto the landing. Steadily she moved her eye over each and every Crash Test Dummy. She had already achieved something with the Thors never possible with the Hybrids. Order. Perfect uniformed order. The room was full of dummies, yet completely silent. All ready to serve. All ready to complete their duty to CrashCorp.

Lucinda took a deep breath and enjoyed the moment.

"Tonight, Thors, you will take control," Lucinda said into the microphone clipped to her ear. "For years we've had to work with the Hybrids. They once claimed the title of being the best Crash Test Dummies in the world. But there is always room for improvement. And the impressive dummies I see before me are that remarkable improvement. A new generation of Crash Test Dummies to lead us into the future.

"This is not simply a matter of taking your rightful place, but a matter of fighting for it. This is your time. Hybrids are now obsolete. Yet, they still mar our presence, filling a position which they're no longer entitled."

Thors felt a uniform sense of power. Many envisioned

their future unfolding before them. They had all come off the same production line, equal in ability. Together they would remain united until they forged a place for themselves at CrashCorp.

"You must know your enemy," Lucinda's voice echoed. "The Hybrids are what stops you from progressing. Until all the Hybrids are gone from CrashCorp, Thors cannot take their rightful place. Slowly, but surely, all Hybrids will be removed and we will step into a new age of Crash Test enlightenment.

"Dummies. There are those who deserve to rule, and those who need to be ruled. You must choose which category you wish to claim as your own. You are the new generation. You will be a strong generation who will outshine all those who have come before. You will live on forever. Your journey will not end at CrashCorp. Once you have achieved your goal of becoming the best Crash Test Dummy possible, you will achieve the status of hero. To reflect the true worthiness of the position, you will claim your place in Elcycer, the Land of Heroes."

Lucinda scanned the Thors. She wondered if any dummies were holding back smiles. If any felt any true emotion, they were keeping it very well contained.

"Thors, take your positions. Graduation is about to begin."

The Thors moved to the edges of the crash test arena and spaced themselves equal distances apart. Lucinda admired their efficiency.

"Open the doors," Lucinda instructed, with a wave of an

arm. Two dummies marched to the doors and pulled them open.

The Hybrids barged into the crash arena. Noisy chatter and laughter filled the arena. Four dummies made their way onto the makeshift stage. Standing before the shrinking group of their colleagues, the graduates lapped up the applause.

Crash performances had ceased. Humans were no longer invited. Light shows didn't fire up. Every ceremony became a little more downgraded than the last. Still, the Hybrids celebrated the departure of their friends to what they believed would be a better place.

Thors watched carefully to make sure the Hybrids didn't get too rowdy.

Lucinda placed one hand on the control desk and held the other in the air.

"May I have your attention? Nothing pleases me more than when we can honour those who have given their all to ensure the safety of others. Your work has made sure billions of people are safe. You all deserve respect for just being here.

"Heroes stand before you. True heroes. Bound for Elcycer. This particular crew has been exemplary in their performance and dedication. Best of the best. They have displayed their brilliance in the art of crashing. Tonight, you will join Elcycer."

The Hybrids erupted and cheered as a Thor presented each graduate with a medal; the same medal presented to Sebastian and the other dummies. Unlike their Thor counterparts, the Hybrids did not try and contain their pride, but felt free to express it. One Hybrid in the audience approached a Thor guarding the perimeter.

"Hey, new guy. Don't forget this is a celebration," he said, slapping the Thor's arm.

"Control your behaviour, or it will be controlled for you," said the Thor.

The Hybrid turned to a friend. "The new guys are certainly a lot of laughs."

"Dummies," said Lucinda, "the night is yours. Enjoy it as though it is your last."

Lucinda turned away from the observation deck, and the glass doors hissed closed as she disappeared.

23

Sebastian stepped inside the children's sleeping quarters. His companions followed. An eerie quiet made the empty room feel abandoned. Names of each of the children had been stencilled onto the walls above where they slept. He walked over to Madison's corner and pulled a picture she had drawn off the wall. In colourful crayon they were all together, smiling. Jupiter held Sebastian's hand, and Madison held her mother's. In another drawing they all smiled out from the windows of a car as it hurtled towards a concrete barrier.

"All the children are gone," said Sebastian mournfully.

Sebastian placed his hand over his mouth. He felt the same kind of dread and helplessness as when he had entered the shipping container. It was if, once again, all his efforts had come too late.

"I don't understand," said Sid. "Madison should be

here."

Sebastian looked across the room. Jupiter's place had been cleaned out. The pictures on the walls and his toys were all gone. Only his stencilled name and the suspension hook used to hold him upright as he slept remained.

Sebastian thought about the last time he saw Jupiter. How Jupiter had held out his hand from the back of the truck as Sebastian chased after it. How he had waited to see Jupiter again at Elcycer, not expecting to find the horror that he did. His artificial heart felt heavy as he imagined the same fate had awaited Madison. Sounds of children once filled the room. At night their laughter would echo down the corridors, even though the humans had told them repeatedly to go to sleep. Sometimes Sebastian would wake up to find Madison had snuck out of the children's quarters, and found her asleep at his feet. But, now there was increasingly little sign they had ever existed at CrashCorp.

"Maybe we shouldn't have come here," said Max. "We should go."

"Why would they throw her away, she was just a kid?" said Sebastian.

Max took Sebastian by the hand. "I don't think it's safe to stay here. Maybe we should leave the factory and try to find another way to help."

"Like what?" said Sebastian. "By then there might be no one left."

"We can take you and Sid to the media," said Max. "With Sid to back you up, they will have to listen to us."

"I couldn't possibly go in front of a camera," said Sid. "I'm far too shy."

"Max, they've already made Sebastian out to look like the bad guy. We'll probably now get charged with breaking into CrashCorp. And stealing their property," Layla said, pointing to Sebastian and Sid.

Sebastian stared towards the ground. CrashCorp once held everything a Crash Test Dummy was made for. Now it had become a wasteland of dreams and the fertile ground of nightmares.

Sebastian looked at everyone. "I'm going in."

"Where?" asked Max.

"I'm going to crash the graduation. Let them know the truth about Elcycer. Tell them the truth about the outside world."

"Sebastian," said Sid. "You don't understand. The Thors won't like it. They will tear you limb from limb."

"What they have waiting for us at Elcycer is much worse," said Sebastian. "We have to get you humans out of here. Sid, you should leave with them."

"Oh, thank goodness. I'm really not the fighting kind. Some of us are forged by a much gentler hand."

Exiting the children's quarters, Sebastian carefully slid the door closed.

"Sleep tight," Sebastian whispered.

Pressing a finger to his lips for everyone to be quiet, Sebastian led them down the corridor. Reaching a corner, he peeked around to make sure no one approached.

"I'll get you guys outside. You'll have to find your own

way after that," said Sebastian.

"I want to stay and help," said Layla.

"This is my world. It can be dangerous for humans."

"But, I've got equipment, I can—"

Sebastian clasped his hand over Layla's mouth, perhaps a little too hard. Everyone snapped still and listened.

Footsteps echoed through the darkened corridors. It was impossible to tell which direction they were coming from. A faint scraping sound accompanied each step. Max and Layla's heart began to race. The Hybrids' hearts would have done the same if it were possible.

Singing. Faint. But, singing.

"Humpty Dumpty sat on a wall. Humpty Dumpty had a great fall."

Sebastian's eyes widened. He looked at Sid.

"All the king's horses and all the king's men . . ."

At the far end of the corridor a figure emerged. It was a small child holding a plastic doll by the hair, dragging it along the floor.

"Madison!" said Sebastian.

". . . couldn't put Humpty together again."

Sebastian began running towards her, the others followed close behind.

Madison reeled backwards, ready to run away.

"Madison," said Sebastian. "It's me."

Madison looked up. "Daddy?"

He stood still and waited for her to come closer.

"Are you okay?" Sebastian asked, holding out his arms to her. Picking her up, he gave her a hug.

"I can't find mummy. She's gone on a walk," said Madison.

Cautiously, not to scare Madison, the others approached.

Madison squirmed in Sebastian's arms. She wanted down.

She walked over to Layla and held up her doll.

"Beep Beep has a sore eye," Madison said, pointing to where the plastic human-like eye once was. Beep Beep also had only one leg and patches of her hair had come out. Max recognised the doll.

"I know that doll," said Max, "what's left of it. It belonged to Ruby."

Layla glanced back to Max.

"Where did you get Beep Beep from?" asked Layla.

"A person-man gave her to me," Madison whispered to Layla.

"My dad," Max said to himself.

"Maybe we could take her to a doctor and get her fixed up," said Layla. "Would you like that?"

"You're pretty," said Madison, staring at Layla.

"Thanks. You too."

"Are you a mummy?" Madison asked.

"No," Layla smiled.

"You look like a mummy."

"You are so sweet, Madison."

Madison squealed in delight. As a sign of affection she head-butted Layla in the face, like she used to do with her mother. Layla fell back on the floor, her backpack cushioning her fall. Clutching her face, Layla pulled her hand away to check if her nose was bleeding. It wasn't. She looked at Madison with surprise and laughed. Not just an ordinary laugh, but a loud braying laugh which closely mimicked the sound of an excited donkey.

Madison looked up as though she was about to cry.

"Honey, it's okay," said Layla. "It didn't hurt too much."

Madison pointed. "It's them."

Turning, they saw three Thors blocking the corridor.

"It's time to graduate."

The Thors grabbed Max and Layla. Their strength was too great for the humans. Madison dropped her doll as a Thor swept her up and clutched her under his arms. Far from being the hero he doubted he would ever be, Sid crumpled in fear.

Sebastian took hold of Madison's hand as she screamed, attempting to pull her free.

"Dad."

Losing his grip, Sebastian fell backwards, as he noticed more Thors advancing. His feet slipping on the concrete floor, Sebastian spun around and fled.

24

Sprinting along the corridor, in the true clumsy Crash Test Dummy fashion, Sebastian pushed open the door to the crash test arena. The swing of the doors gained everyone's immediate attention. In unison, Thors turned their heads and took an authoritarian stance.

"You have to listen to me," Sebastian yelled. "Elcycer doesn't exist. They're sending you away to become spare parts."

Having expected his colleagues to react with shock and anger, Sebastian was dumbfounded when they looked back at him equally as dumbfounded.

"Sebastian?" said a Hybrid. "What are you doing back?"

"It's all a lie. You're being sent to your death," said Sebastian.

"Death?" said another Hybrid.

"Where's death?" asked a teenage Hybrid.

"Never heard of it," muttered another.

"They're trying to get rid of us. We're not heroes. We're future spare parts. No one outside the factory even knows we exist," said Sebastian.

"Of course we're heroes, Sebastian. Just look at us."

"We need to escape," yelled Sebastian. "There's a whole world out there where we can be free. It goes all the way to the bridge."

"Are you just making things up?" asked a female Hybrid.

Confusion and murmuring swept through the dummies.

The glass doors hissed as Lucinda re-emerged on the balcony. Her eyes tightened as she locked on Sebastian, like a cruise missile fixing on its target. Some Hybrids turned to Lucinda, unsure what to do. Lucinda looked to Burnside, the head Thor, and gave a slight nod.

"Dummies remain calm," said Lucinda. "This situation is easy to explain. Sebastian is defective. Something we thought better to keep confidential, out of respect for Sebastian. We felt it safer if he was removed from the testing program. For that reason he has not reached Elcycer. Because he cannot accept his own failings, he wishes everyone else to also fail. What you see before you is a dummy gone mad. A traitor. You all must stop him. Use any means necessary. Thors, you know what to do."

The Thors marched forward and formed a barricade between the Hybrids and Sebastian. A group of Thors circled Sebastian. Two Thors pulled the doors closed and guarded them. Sebastian glanced around for an escape route, but every direction was blocked.

His only option was to fight. Lowering his head, he lunged forward and crashed into two dummies. They fell to the floor. Sebastian tumbled on top of them. Other Thors pounced. He became lost under an avalanche of hard robotic bodies. Trying to push his way up, he was pinned back against the floor. In the frantic scuffle, he felt himself being pulled in all directions. His shoulder snapped as he felt his arm become dislocated. The last thing he saw was his own arm coming down as it struck him in the head. It was like Lord of the Crash Test Dummies.

Everything went black for Sebastian.

The whole arena watched as he was dragged away. His body limp. His head tilting down. The doors clicked closed.

"Due to the interruption, graduation will conclude early this evening," said Lucinda. "Graduates will be transported to Elcycer. The factory will go into lock down. All Hybrids are to return to your holding quarters."

Lucinda turned, exiting the arena.

The Thors stepped forward, herding the Hybrids towards the centre of the arena. A confused Hybrid moved a little too slow and felt a solid push in the back. "Who made them the boss of everything?" he said, feeling another shove.

The exit doors opened.

"March," yelled Burnside. The Thors formed a physical wall as they moved the Hybrids out.

From the stage, the four graduating dummies were led down the ramp and into the network of florescent-lit corridors. Their footsteps sounded in rhythm as they were funnelled along the snake-like corridors, following the same path all other dummies who had left the factory had marched. Heading towards Elcycer. Heading to become heroes.

"But we didn't even get our photo," said a Hybrid. "What if Sebastian was right? He wanted to go to Elcycer more than anyone."

"Don't worry about it," replied another. "Sebastian's just smashed his head too many times. Where as we have a smashing time ahead."

Not entirely convinced, the Hybrid kept up with his fellow Crash Test Dummies and trudged towards the loading bay.

25

Lucinda travelled through CrashCorp on an electric trolley with Burnside in the passenger seat and two Thors in the back. They whizzed passed glowing nightlights running along the floor. After waiting so long to find Sebastian, and enduring the negative publicity he had brought CrashCorp, he had finally returned home, delivering himself to her.

"What do you have to report?" Lucinda asked.

"We have the rogue dummy in a holding cell," said Burnside. "He is being guarded. The graduating dummies are being loaded onto the truck for transport as we speak."

"Have the other Hybrids settled down?"

"Currently contained in their quarters. They were easy to control."

"Hopefully we can finally put this trouble to bed," said Lucinda.

"We've also apprehended two small humans. We believe

they've been helping Sebastian on the outside, and broke in to help the other Hybrids escape," said Burnside.

"Really?" Lucinda locked on the Thors, hiding her amazement. "They're inside the facility?"

"We found the small humans with two dummies," said Burnside. "Sid – the scared one, and Madison – a child Hybrid. Looks like they were attempting to escape."

"Where are they now?" asked Lucinda.

"They're being detained in an unused storage room. Should we alert the human authorities?"

"No," Lucinda paused to think. "They entered my turf, I will deal with them personally. Make sure the truck to Elcycer is kept in the dock until I give clearance for it to leave. They may be taking a couple of extra passengers."

Stopping outside a storage room, Thors stepped off the trolley and ripped open the door. They stepped aside as Lucinda entered.

Two Thors stood on either side of Sebastian. Hanging from the ceiling, by a steel cable and hook through the top of his head, Sebastian hung with his feet hovering above the concrete floor. Sebastian's arm lay discarded under his feet, the arm of his overalls hanging loose by his side.

"Thank you, Thors. I would like a few moments alone," said Lucinda.

The Thors left, sealing the door behind them.

Sebastian looked terrified as Lucinda paced around and examined him. He tried to follow her with his eyes, but found himself unable to move, and she stepped behind him and out of view.

"You've certainly not kept yourself up to the standards we expect from CrashCorp dummies," said Lucinda, eyeing his many scuffmarks. "The outside world mustn't have treated you very well."

"They didn't send me to be recycled."

"These . . . kids. The ones who have been harbouring you. How many people have they told that you're their new pet?"

"They are none of your business," stuttered Sebastian.

"Oh, I think they are. You see, when a dummy escapes from my facility and kidnaps two children, I think it's very much my business. Who's going to think of you as a hero now, Sebastian?"

"I didn't kidnap Max and Layla," said Sebastian. "They showed me how you were turning us into spare parts. Elcycer is a lie."

"Max and Layla. So we finally have some names."

Sebastian was frustrated he had given their names away, and tried to jerk himself free.

Lucinda stood directly in front of him. She picked up his arm off the floor and held it up with both hands for him to see.

"Understand Sebastian, the great thing about Crash Test Dummies is that they're completely disposable. Once we've finished with them, it's a simple matter of taking them apart piece by piece, until they're nothing more than a collection of basic components."

"That's not right," said Sebastian. "We're real."

"Yes, you are," said Lucinda. "But for a limited time

only."

Sebastian kicked as he tried in vain to break free.

"After awarding you so many opportunities, you try sabotaging our operation, all because you were so naïve to believe a little fib about Elcycer. Hardly my fault if you believe a lie. I trust you had fun on the outside. You certainly garnered yourself a lot of attention and caused us all kinds of headaches. It is not something we take lightly."

Her heels clinking on the floor, Lucinda moved behind Sebastian.

"Who else on the outside knows about you?"

Sebastian remained quiet and stared directly ahead.

"Not talking? I'm sure your little friends — Max and Layla — will be a lot more cooperative." She moved around to watch Sebastian's reaction. "What exactly did you think you were going to achieve with your display at graduation? After all, you are just a dummy."

Holding Sebastian's arm out in front of him, Lucinda dropped it at his feet. She smiled

"I believe no one knows either you or your little friends are here. It's not like you are going to go around blabbing about your plans. For all anyone knows, a deranged Crash Test Dummy could have kidnapped them. I hope they're careful in such a big factory. CrashCorp is a dangerous place and they could easily get themselves in some kind of accident."

Sebastian tried to wiggle free, pulling on the cable with his arm. He weighed too much to lift himself. Lucinda turned and walked towards the door. She opened it as

Sebastian struggled.

"Sebastian," Lucinda crooked her head back. "If you think being recycled is so bad, perhaps you should consider where some of your spare parts came from when you were reassembled after crashing. You can hardly claim yourself to be innocent in all of this."

The door slammed shut, leaving Sebastian alone with the silence.

Lucinda drove the trolley back to her office and poured herself another coffee. It was going to be a long night.

On her computer she searched the updated news coverage.

"Police are currently searching for the missing teenagers . . ."

"The police air wing helicopters are involved . . ."

"Social media networks have flared up with many people stating their fears for the missing pair and hoping for their safe return . . ."

Searching through the social networking sites Lucinda thanked the internet for not being very good at keeping secrets. She read through some of the messages:

- *Max was suspended for trashing the school with a ride-on lawnmower.*

- *I'm Layla's best friend at school and it's tragic what's happening. Safe home babe.*

- *Max ran away so many times he didn't finish the school year then dropped out.*

"This kids a real tearaway," said Lucinda to herself. Glancing down the page she noticed their names.

- Max Alderson and Layla Ramos kidnapped by a Crash Test Dummy! WTF!

- Max's dad and sister were killed in a car accident last year, here's the article . . .

Lucinda read the article, stood up from her desk, walked over to the window, and spent a few moments contemplating.

*　　　*　　　*

It was hard to say how long they had been held. Max had nodded off several times. He tried to force himself to stay awake, but sleep found a way to take over. Hours passed. He had grown thirsty, but the mechanical captors didn't understand the human need for water. Layla slept with her head on his shoulder.

Max checked his phone to see if there was any coverage. Yet again, there was none. He watched as the door opened and he nudged Layla awake.

Max, Layla and Sid sat on a bench along the wall. Madison sat on the floor, one hand holding onto Layla's leg, the other playing with her doll. Two Thors watched over them, silently commanding them to be quiet. Terrified, Sid gripped Max's hand a lot harder than humans felt comfortable with.

Lucinda entered with Burnside, the door sliding open with a bang.

"Remove the dummies," ordered Lucinda.

The Thors stepped forward and seized Sid. He flinched.

Max pulled the phone from his shorts pocket and slipped it into Sid's overalls.

"Find a way," Max said to Sid.

A solid forearm of a Thor pushed against Max's throat, holding him against the wall. He tried to breathe, but could only feel his throat sticking together. He clawed at the arm with his fingers.

Sid was yanked forward, causing him to fall. Thors clutched his ankles, spun him around and dragged him out the door.

Reaching down, a Thor eyed Madison and grabbed her shoulder. Madison dug her fingers into Layla's leg. As the Thor tugged harder, Madison's grip tightened, not realising she would bruise Layla's leg. Layla snatched Madison's arms. She didn't care about bruising — rock climbing had taught her pain never lasts and bruises always fade — all she cared about was saving Madison.

Layla pulled Madison closer as the Thor tried to drag her off.

"Hold on, Madison."

Lucinda's hand slapped Layla hard across the face. Stars. Confusion. Stars. Madison's hands slipped away. The door closed. Madison and Sid were gone. Layla regained focus.

Max shook as he tried to control his breathing.

"Max Alderson," said Lucinda. "I remember your father Daniel."

Max's eyes slowly moved up from the floor to meet Lucinda's.

"We had contact with him for a while, he showed us his designs for a new energy system for cars. But, at CrashCorp we're about quality, not quantity. We were developing the exact same product at the exact same time. Just one of those synchronicities of the Universe, I suppose. A remarkable coincidence. We were worried that he might have stolen our ideas, trying to claim them as his own."

Max remembered how his father would spend nights explaining his work to his mother. Max never quite understood. He remembered how his father talked about something he had invented that would make them rich. How their family would benefit for years to come. All the years of work and hardship would pass and his ideas would change everything.

"What struck me about your father was that he was only ever interested in himself. What was in it for him. The last thing we needed was some upstart waltzing in and claiming all the credit. I, on the other hand, like to look at the bigger picture," said Lucinda.

Confusion took over Max. This is not how he remembered his father. His father had always looked out for others. At the funeral, many people read eulogies and spoke of how he had helped them, and how his potential had been cut short. Max watched a video of the funeral in the weeks after he woke from his coma.

"The solar powered paint he *inspired* took us in directions we never anticipated. It was such a pity to hear about the accident."

Max glared at her.

"Accidents are our speciality after all," said Lucinda. "But, sometimes they just can't be helped. Unfortunate really, but any time something big like this comes along there's always a little collateral damage, necessary to protect the greater good."

Max felt his body begin to tremble and his mind turned blank. Flashes of the car accident lit up in his mind. The crash. The car spinning. Metal grinding. Shattered glass appeared as though it was suspended in mid-air. Seeing the car tyre spin as he lay on the road. The feet as they awkwardly ran away, as he blacked out. The feet. The shape of the driver running. This image now seemed more familiar. It wasn't a drunk driver. It was a Crash Test Dummy.

Max stared at Lucinda in terror.

"Max?" said Layla. "What's she talking about?"

Lucinda gave a smug smile. "I don't know exactly what you were trying to achieve by coming here. Still, you can explain everything to the police when they arrive. I'm sure they will be more than happy to listen. Especially to someone with your . . . *history.*"

Max's eyes dropped to the floor.

"Don't worry, child," said Lucinda. "I won't involve the police. I'm sure a rebel like you would prefer something a bit more adventurous. I don't know, something like going for a joyride, wrapping a car around a tree. Just a couple more victims, adding to the road toll we work so tirelessly to keep down. You might even be lucky and end up in the newspapers. I can see the headlines now, 'Joyriding Teens in Fatal Tragedy'. Just another accident. Like father, like son."

"Why are you doing this?" said Max.

"It's not about *why*," said Lucinda. "It's about *what*. What are you going to do about it? And don't bother about trying to phone for help. Signal jammers surround the facility. Wouldn't want anything getting out that shouldn't."

Lucinda left and Burnside secured the door.

Alone in the room, Max looked across to Layla.

"I don't think I should have brought you here."

26

Twisting his wrists behind his back, Thors marched Sid through the corridors. Madison kicked and punched and screamed, but her little body had no impact on the Thor carrying her. Her screams echoed in the dimly lit passages. Sid was terrified, more than usual.

"I don't want to be recycled," he shrieked.

"Nothing these old Hybrids say makes sense," said the Thor in a monotone voice.

"I want my mum," screamed Madison.

Sid tried to pull away, but the Thors' hold was too strong. Used to being in situations he didn't want to be in, Sid had perfected a stalling technique. He had discovered a secret move, particularly effective when humans tried to order him onto the crash floor. The level of mastermind and cunning he had developed was so unique that others rarely saw it coming.

Sid pretended to faint.

Lying on the ground, the Thor kicked Sid. "Get up." He kicked again.

"Don't," yelled Madison.

Frustrated, the Thor took Sid under the armpits and tried to lift him. The Thor's hand slipped and Sid's face smashed on the floor.

"We have a real hero with this one, don't we?" said the Thor.

Madison squirmed, almost tumbling from the Thor's grip. He used his elbow to hook her around the neck. He pulled her back under his arm with no more care than if he was carrying a bag of potatoes.

Clutching Sid's limp hand, the Thor gave a sigh.

"It's little wonder this model is obsolete," said the Thor.

Sid felt the strong desire to retort, but contained himself, afraid of blowing his cover.

The Thor dragged Sid along the floor. Sid opened one eye slightly, watching the feet of the Thor holding Madison. Besides fainting formulating part one of his plans, Sid hadn't come up with any following steps. With humans, he could enjoy their frustration, as the crash test would be delayed, often for hours, while he stalled. If he was lucky, a crash could be postponed for days until it could be rescheduled. But this time he couldn't afford any delays.

With a twist of his wrist, Sid broke free. Spinning his body around, he kicked out the feet of both Thors. They fell. Finally, Sid had found a kind of crash he enjoyed.

Madison flew from the Thor's hold and hit the wall before crashing down. Sid scurried to his feet.

Gripping Madison's hand, Sid ran in the direction they had come. Jolting back, Sid turned. A Thor had snatched Madison by her other arm. Staggering, Sid looked back. He had lost Madison. The other Thor rose to his feet. Sid panicked and ran and ran and ran.

"Leave him," heard Sid. "We'll send some troops after him. He can't get far."

Sid ran until all he heard was his own footsteps. Stopping, he listened, hearing Madison screaming, until he heard nothing. Sid knew he was no hero. He was exactly what others told him he was. He was a failure. Defective. Only good for spare parts.

Walking only on what should be his toes, if Crash Test Dummies had toes, Sid made his way to an unused storage room. Gently he opened the door a sliver, squeezed himself through, and closed it without making a sound.

"Sid!" a voice boomed.

Sid squealed like . . . well . . . a little girl . . . like Madison to be exact. Spinning around, he pushed his back against the door and almost truly fainted. His computerised heart was almost about to short circuit.

Sid saw Sebastian suspended from the ceiling.

"My old buddy," smiled Sebastian.

"My delicate nerves," said Sid.

"Where are the others?" Sebastian asked.

"Sebastian, please don't hate me."

"Hate you? There's no one else in the world I would

more like to run down with a prime mover."

"They have Madison. I tried to save her, but she slipped away."

Sebastian's face dropped. "Who has Madison?"

"The new ones. I really tried but I got scared." Sid fell to his knees and put his hands over his face. "They took us away from Max and Layla. But Max gave me this. I don't even know what it is." Sid handed the phone over to Sebastian.

"An oracle," gasped Sebastian.

"Why do humans make everything so complicated?" Sid felt a panic attack coming on. It gathered full speed. "All I want is a little peace. Just to be left alone . . . where I don't crash into things, and people don't crash things into me. Is it really too much to ask for? It would be so much easier for everyone." Sid crumpled over and blubbered on the floor in a way only a Crash Test Dummy could blubber.

"When you're done, can you unhook me, please?"

Nervous, Sid rose to his feet. Holding Sebastian around the waist, Sid lifted him up. Sebastian used his free arm to unhook himself. Sid lowered Sebastian to the ground – or rather dropped him on the ground. Sebastian picked up his arm and reattached it.

"That feels better."

Taking the phone from Sid's quivering hand, Sebastian touched the screen and the photos from the recycling yard appeared.

"We have to show the others," said Sebastian.

"Can't we just stay here?" asked Sid. "We can hide, like

old times."

"Soon there will be no old times," said Sebastian. "They can't just treat us like a bunch of dummies. We have to be heroes."

"I've heard there's a thing called pizza. Apparently it's really good. Let's see if we can find some of that instead."

Dropping the phone into his pocket Sebastian grabbed Sid. Pushing the door open they ran towards the Hybrids' sleeping quarters. Sebastian ran with determination, whereas Sid followed gaining a sense of foreboding with each step.

Entering the sleeping quarters, the Hybrids all turned.

"Look," said a Hybrid. "It's Mr Damaged and Mr Deranged."

"Come to save us again, have you Sebastian?" laughed another.

He looked at the dummies, all suspended from the ceiling, their feet barely touching the ground. The once full room now only housed several dummies. He noticed his old hook and realised how much he had changed since leaving CrashCorp. These dummies had no idea of the outside world and what awaited them. In reality there was not much waiting for them at all. They still had dreams of Elcycer and believed they would get there some day – the sooner the better.

"I have to show you all something," said Sebastian.

"Sorry, but this space is reserved for heroes," a Hybrid sneered.

"Elcycer doesn't exist."

"What would you know about Elcycer? You obviously weren't hero enough to get there."

The last remaining dummies laughed at Sebastian.

Lifting up the phone, Sebastian flashed it in the closest Hybrid's face. He showed her a photo taken inside the shipping container. A photo of Astrid. A photo of the spare parts they would become. Her body slumped and she stopped laughing. Her jaw fell open. Other dummies kept laughing.

"Guys, this isn't funny," she said, stunned.

Sebastian moved along to each dummy to show them the pictures. Each reacted the same. One-by-one the dummies saw their ever-approaching future. The imaginary world of Elcycer shattered.

"This oracle shows us what we will become," said Sebastian.

With arms flailing, the dummies looked as though they were fighting with themselves as they tried to unclasp their suspension hooks.

"We need to escape the factory. We have to help the others before they are trucked away," said Sebastian, helping his fellow dummies down.

"How about I just wait here, and I will catch up with you guys later?" said Sid.

*   *   *

Lucinda stood on the platform overlooking the crash test floor. The EnviroCar was positioned, with the propulsion cables attached to pull it along the crash floor and towards the undercarriage of a truck; designed to test if the accident would cause decapitation of the occupants in the upcoming model. The crash had been planned for the following day to trial the first Thor. Circumstances had changed. A new car would be found for that crash. By morning no evidence would remain of the unscheduled test about to occur.

Max screamed as a Thor pulled him towards the car. Layla was behind him doing the same. Max knew they were going to force him into the car, the same way the police had done. In the backseat he thought he saw Ruby already strapped in. Swinging his body to break free, Max no longer cared if he was injured. He felt a sharp swipe to the side of his head, and air being trapped in his lungs as a Thor gripped him around the neck. Max fought, but the fight began to leave him. He felt dizzy and confused. It wasn't Ruby in the backseat. It was Madison. He wanted to save her, but the Thor's strangle hold was too strong.

Max's eyes jittered as he woke. Floodlights burned down. He didn't know how long he had been out. Something felt familiar and uncomfortable.

A seatbelt. He felt sick. With a heady glare, he turned. Layla was crying, strapped awkwardly into the seat with her backpack pushing behind her.

I didn't know Layla could cry, Max thought.

He saw the steering wheel and the dashboard, and beyond the window was a space that ended with the rear end section of a semi-trailer.

"It's time to tidy up all the loose ends," Lucinda smiled to Burnside.

Max looked to Layla. He couldn't make words. Tears pushed from his eyes. His throat choked. He wanted to say, *I'm sorry*. Max felt faint. Images of the car crash with his family sped through his mind. He knew the sound it would make, the destruction it would cause. He didn't want Layla to experience this. He wanted to be back in the treehouse. He wanted to be safe.

"I want to remember this moment," said Lucinda.

The high-definition slow-motion cameras began recording. Lucinda pressed the starter button. The car accelerated.

27

It sounded like a little earthquake. Rumbling. Crashing. Silence. Rumbling. Then another crash. The doors bulged, being forced from the outside. Metal hinges cringed under the pressure. Buckling, the locks broke. Crash Test Dummies poured onto the crash test floor, falling over each other.

The wheels of the EnviroCar spun forward as it accelerated. The sound of the uninvited Hybrids drowned out the screams of the EnviroCar's occupants.

Lucinda crooked her neck. The dummies had infiltrated the arena. She was not concerned. After all they were just dummies. Mere dummies.

"The Hybrids are revolting," said Burnside.

Lucinda snorted, self-assured their attempts would be futile. Camera flashes lit up the crash floor, recording as the vehicle careened towards obliteration.

Confused by the lights and the movement, Max still knew what was coming. He reached across the backseat and took Madison's hand. Inertia pushed Max against the seat. For a moment he relaxed, appreciating what it felt like to be human. It was the only thing he could control. His mind washed with images of his father and his family, and how they were once all happy together. Max held the moment because he knew very soon it was going to hurt. A lot. Or possibly he would never hurt again. He wanted to stay suspended in the moment forever.

Sebastian pushed Sid through the glass doors. It was more spur of the moment rather than a plan. Glass shattered, spraying the balcony and causing it to rain to the crash floor.

Sid collided with Lucinda. Her face hit the control deck and she fell to the floor.

Sid grappled to regain his feet, slipping on the shattered glass.

Sebastian leapt over them both. His fist punched the control button.

The car stopped with a sharp jolt.

Max would have screamed if he felt capable. Layla stared forward. She had expected the worst, and thought about how her parents would feel if they never saw her again. They both looked up in a daze, seeing the edge of the trailer just a breath from the windscreen.

Burnside punched Sid in the face. He fell. Focusing his attention on Sebastian, the Thor launched into the air. Sebastian grabbed his own wrist and dislodged his arm.

With a forceful swing, Sebastian's arm connected with Burnside's head. Lucinda ducked, barely missing being hit.

Lucinda wiped blood from her nose as she sprinted over broken glass. Arms appeared, blocking her escape. Two Hybrids stepped in front of her. Crash Test Dummies never had much of an understanding for hair and it was the first place they grabbed Lucinda.

Hybrids surged to free the trio from the car. In a coordinated movement, Thors aligned themselves in attack mode. In a fierce mess of limbs and clashing of bodies, a Hybrid was hurled into the air and came plummeting down to the ground. Thors overpowered the Hybrids, forming a barricade around the car. All the occupants screamed as bodies bounced over the roof and across the bonnet.

A roar like thunder reverberated from outside. A rattle of metal echoed across the crash test arena. The roller door at the end of the room bulged forward and rippled upwards as it was torn from the base. Full-beam headlights glared as a truck hurtled across the crash test arena, tyres squealing on the floor. Swerving, the truck tilted as the Hybrid driver aimed at the Thors. The truck bounced as it barrelled over their bodies. Others flew off the sides, rolling into clumsy heaps.

Turning the steering wheel a hard-left, and slamming on the brakes, the truck spun around. The doors on the back flung open, catapulting Hybrids across the arena and towards the car. It was an unexpected detour on the way to Elcycer.

The Hybrids descended on the car. Pulling the doors open, they helped Max, Layla and Madison unbuckled their restraints and cleared a path for them to run free.

Holding Lucinda firmly by her arms, two Hybrids directed her towards the vehicle. She glared around, wild-eyed, blood dripping from her nose.

"You can't do this," Lucinda screamed.

Thors tried to block the car, but the Hybrids surged forward, pushing them away.

With a final heave Lucinda was forced into the driver's seat. The restraints tightened across her chest and around her waist. A Hybrid squeezed the belt buckle, bending it, to stop her releasing it.

Thors found themselves barricaded behind a chain of Hybrids.

Pushing on the hood, Hybrids reversed the car along the crash floor, placing it back into the starting position. Sebastian watched from the control platform.

Looking around in the confusion, Max turned and ran across the arena.

"Max?" Layla yelled. "Where're you going?"

"Look after Madison," called Max, as he ran out through a door.

With the car in place, Sebastian pushed the starter button. The pulley whizzed as the car rushed forward. Lucinda focused on the truck trailer zooming up to her. Her face contorted in horror.

"We're going to have a crash," said Burnside.

For a moment the Thors forgot about their allegiance to

Lucinda in exchange for witnessing their first crash test.

Max ran up the corridor and scuttled over the broken glass.

"We can't do this." Max pushed Sebastian aside.

He slammed his fist down, hitting the kill switch. The EnviroCar ground to a halt. Lucinda lurched forward and her mouth filled with vomit. Some spilt out. She convulsed as she tried to catch her breath and swallow the coffee tasting sick. She spluttered, relieved the crash had been aborted.

"I thought you'd like this," said Sebastian.

"This won't fix anything," said Max. "It will just make things worse."

Max picked up the headset and put it on.

"Don't worry," Max's voice echoed across the arena. "You'll have to live with what you've done."

28

Sebastian felt something not previously recorded in dummy history. A surge of energy took over his whole body, buzzing right throughout his circuitry. The energy moved down his spine, through his shoulders, into his arms, and at the same time it hit his feet. It was an inexplicable feeling. For the first time Sebastian felt as though he was similar to the humans. He felt alive.

Standing next to Max, Sebastian looked over the arena where he had performed his most crowd-pleasing crashes; where he watched and encouraged others to become heroes. He now wore the spare parts of his fellow Hybrids. Lucinda was right. Sebastian did have his part in their demise, cheering them towards their *destiny*. He had almost turned Lucinda into spare parts, and his churning anger almost made him become just like her.

"I'm made to save lives, not to destroy them," Sebastian

realised.

The crash arena appeared different to how he remembered. Not just because he viewed it from another angle, or that it was littered with a brilliant chaos, but somehow it felt unfamiliar, as though it was no longer his home.

He watched Lucinda wrestle with her seatbelt. She tried to struggle free, but found herself trapped.

Sebastian took the microphone from Max.

"Outside the factory is a place much greater than anything they promised us here."

The Hybrids gazed up at him. "There's a place where we can be free. Bigger than the Elcycer we imagine. There's a greater world out there full of humans who don't want to turn us all into spare parts."

Even some Thors looked up to Sebastian to consider what he said.

"They have trained us to believe CrashCorp is all there is. Lucinda wants you to believe that, because it makes things easier for her. We have to show the world we're not just a bunch of dummies."

Hybrids looked at each other, unsure if that last statement was correct.

"Just because he's done with all his crashing, he doesn't think we should have our turn," a Thor called out.

"We have to run," yelled Sid. "We have to escape from this place. Whatever's out there must be more fun than this."

Thors straightened up and twisted their bodies back into

alignment. Cracking joints, they rose to their feet and retrained their focus on the humans and Hybrids. Turning in unison, Thors reverted back to their programming. A group approached Layla, Madison and Sid.

Sebastian felt a tug on his hand.

"We have to leave now," said Max. "Or they'll hunt us down."

Sebastian and Max ran along the corridor and down the stairs.

Max ran too fast for Sebastian to keep up, who tumbled down the stairs and beat Max to the bottom.

Entering the crash arena, Max signalled to Layla.

"Let's go," he called.

Layla took Madison's hand and raced towards the damaged roller door. Thors staggered after them.

Outside the door was a parking lot.

The perimeter fences were high. Even with Layla's abseiling rope it would take too long for the five of them to climb over.

"How do we get out?" Max asked Sebastian.

Near the factory wall a series of the next model of EnviroCars were parked, each awaiting their fate in the crash test arena.

"There," said Layla.

"No way am I getting in one of those," Max said. "I've had enough of cars for one lifetime."

Layla looked at Sebastian. "You're going to have to drive."

"Me?"

"You're the only one who has any experience."

"Sebastian? Are you crazy?" yelled Max. "He only knows how to crash."

"Do you want to do it?" snapped Layla.

Racing towards a car, Sebastian hopped into the driver's seat.

Sid hesitated and glanced at Sebastian, "Just don't do anything crashy. I want to enter the world in one piece."

"Have I ever let you down before?" said Sebastian.

"None of this is good for my constitution," said Sid, covering his face.

Nervously, Sid watched as Thors ran towards them. Against his own better judgement, he jumped in the car. Layla hopped in the backseat with Madison. She looked up to see Max standing, staring at the car, transfixed.

"Max," she yelled, "get in."

Leaning out of the car door, she reached out to Max.

"Please, Max," cried Madison. "They'll catch us."

Max turned to see Thors advancing.

Taking a deep breath, Max climbed inside.

The rising sun streamed trails of bright orange light through the mangled roller door and across the crash floor. Thors stammered. All dummies — Hybrids and Thors — turned to see the sunrise. A brilliant glowing ball crept over the horizon. This was the first view of the outside world they had ever experienced. They were unsure if they should go out into it, or even if they were allowed to.

"What are you waiting for?" Lucinda yelled, still strapped in the car. "Go and get them. The only thing it takes for the Hybrids to win is for Thors to do nothing. Do what you're designed to do, and smash the daylights out of them. If you want your place in Elcycer you will do as you're told."

Burnside turned towards several fully functional Thors.

"You heard her," Burnside yelled. "This is war. Use any means possible."

Some Thors raced towards the electric trollies, as Burnside marched to the truck. Thors loaded into the cabin with him as others clambered into the back. Revving the trucks engine, the wheels screeched on the floor sending up smoke.

"Get me out of here first, you stupid dummies," yelled Lucinda. She watched the truck and the trollies drive away.

The few remaining Hybrids picked their broken bodies up off the crash floor. Not everyone was complete and it was unclear which parts belonged to whom. Limping and unsteady, the Hybrids searched for their body parts. Pulling himself along the ground, a Hybrid picked up an arm belonging to a Thor and clicked it into his hip.

"Hey, nice fit." Standing like some kind of Franken-dummy, he said, "I think it's time we showed Lucinda who's boss."

The Hybrids unhooked the car from its rigging and pushed it away from the trailer. Lucinda unsuccessfully ordered them to stop.

Pressing on the accelerator Sebastian drove an EnviroCar against the heavy gate, attempting to force it open. The gate barely shuddered under the strain of the electric engine.

Max pulled on the door handle and leapt from the car.

"Get back," Max yelled.

"What are you doing?" said Layla.

"Back, back," waved Max.

Sebastian reversed the car into the shadows.

Max stood in front of the gates. Jumping, he threw his arms in the air.

"Hey, over here," he yelled.

From the truck cabin Burnside locked Max in his sights and slammed his foot on the accelerator. The truck charged towards Max like an enraged rhinoceros.

Watching from the shadows Layla, Madison and Sid screamed as the truck focused on Max. Sebastian clapped his hands with excitement, not understanding the full impact of a full impact.

The truck hurtled towards Max. He remembered the headlights approaching from his accident. This time was different. This time he had a chance of escaping.

Max leapt to the side as the truck careened through the gates, breaking one gate from its hinges. It bounced along the street.

As Sebastian drove the car passed, Max leapt through the window and into the backseat.

They escaped from CrashCorp.

29

Brakes hissed as the bus pulled over. Louis knew his route, where every kid should be picked up, and he noticed when any were not waiting at their stop. The children were collected and took their seats on board. Someone had discovered origami and it swept through the bus like a tsunami. As long as the children were occupied Louis didn't have to worry about anyone fighting.

Tyres skidded on the asphalt road, burning rubber. Louis jolted forward in his seat, his stomach pressing hard against the wheel. The children grab the seat in front of them. A red car had cut off the bus, driven by something Louis could only describe as someone in fancy dress. He thought it looked like a Crash Test Dummy, with a backseat full of teenagers. One looked like a girl he used to pick up at the stop on Benz Drive.

"Is everyone okay?" Louis called. He wanted to say

worse things, but the children would hear, followed by the rest of the school, and followed by the principal. Hyperactivity rippled through the bus and Louis knew everyone was fine.

Driving down the centre of the road a truck hurtled passed, narrowly missing the bus.

Lunatics, Louis thought, as he watched the truck swerve along the road.

"I don't like this place that's not the factory," said a Thor to Burnside. "We should go back to CrashCorp and ask Lucinda what to do."

Burnside believed his companion was correct. He realised he had only ever operated by taking instructions and wasn't sure if he could make a decision on his own. And, the red car was already making its way into the distance. Without slowing down enough, Burnside spun the steering wheel to turn the truck around. Speed and sharp turns can be quite a nasty thing, as Burnside discovered. So did the gnomes and topiary animals of Mrs Jessop's lawn, which met their unexpected demise when the truck careened through the front garden and firmly implanted itself in her living room. Thankfully for Mrs Jessop, the only thing occurring in her living room at the time was the recording of her favourite television shows to watch on her return. The recordings didn't survive.

"Great idea!" Burnside blamed his companion as he climbed out the window. Pulling a piece of gnome fragment from his forehead, Burnside stumbled across the busted furniture and through the front yard, tripping over the leafy head of a decapitated giraffe. He watched as the red EnviroCar sped up the hill.

Crash Test Dummies piled out of the back of the truck. Louis watched in astonishment. He pulled his mobile phone from his pocket and tried to call emergency services. Before the call could be placed, a Thor marched towards him and his bus of hyperactive children. Pulling on the door lever, Louis held the door closed.

Burnside's synthetic fists shattered the glass of the bus door, and the strength of the Thors easily forced it open. Louis jumped from his seat to fight them off. His only thought was to protect the children. Secretly, there were a few children he would love to throw to the dummies, but he would have to hear complaints from parents.

Grabbing Louis by his arms and around his neck a Thor pulled him from the bus, and threw him to the ground. Burnside took the driver's seat. Another Thor stormed the bus. Louis tried in vain to get back on before he saw a Crash Test Dummy's fist coming towards his face. Louis saw stars and flashes of white as he hit the ground.

Grinding the gears, the bus bunny-hopped forward.

A Thor stood at the front, placing his hands on the metal railings.

"We are now in control," he yelled. "Sit down. Shut up. Enjoy the ride."

Younger children sat fixed to their seats, too terrified to move, while those further down surged to the back of the bus.

At the end of a street, Burnside slammed his foot on the

brake. The kids flew forward, some falling into the seats in front of them. Nothing was broken. Some found it fun. Most did not.

Burnside checked each way up the road, his foot held strong on the brake. He spotted the direction the EnviroCar had taken.

Burnside slammed his foot on the accelerator. The bus drove over a concrete median island, ripping away the undercarriage. Turning down a street, pieces of the bus fell away, clinking as they dropped onto the road. Fluid splashed onto the asphalt, leaving a Hansel and Gretel trail behind the bus.

Sebastian didn't know which way to look as he drove. There were so many things he could crash in to. A lamppost appeared like a good place to stop. A brick wall looked kind of attractive. An old tree would be a great place to turn this car into a bonfire. For the first time he worried about the companions seated next to him. He resisted the overwhelming urge to crash. He understood humans were quite complicated creatures, who broke easily and were squishy on the inside. In the rearview mirror the bus made a fast approach.

The grill of the bus followed Sebastian along Riverdale Drive until it bumped the back of the car. The bus shoved the car forward. A crash. A different kind of crash. A crash that scared Sebastian.

"Hold on," Sebastian said.

Max crumpled down in the backseat. He felt lightheaded and as though he was going to be sick, but his body was too tense. He knew it was a bad idea to hop in a car again.

Swerving sharply, the bus pulled alongside the car, matching its speed. Sid glanced out the window, seeing Burnside through the broken glass door of the bus.

Sid screamed as the bus scraped along the side of the car. Sparks flared. Everyone screamed. The car swerved over the road as the bus pulled away and swung back for another strike. The car doors buckled. Max threw his body over Madison as the side windows exploded. Layla buried her head between her knees.

Sid became frustrated that even though he had escaped from the factory he was still being subjected to crashes. He smashed the passenger side window with his elbow and lifted himself through the opening.

"He's trying to get on-board." The Thor noticed Sid as he attempted to steady himself on the moving vehicle.

Burnside turned to see Sid climbing out onto the roof. He swung the steering wheel and rammed the car, sending it to the kerb. Sid slipped, his knee cracking the windshield. Sliding across the hood, Sid fell towards the road. His hand latched onto the driver side mirror. His legs hit the asphalt. Trying to run, Sid's feet skipped along the road. Kicking up a leg, he caught it in the window frame of the rear door. Sid pulled himself up, clinging to the side of the car, watching the road beneath him whiz by in a blur.

Looking up, Sid saw the bus returning for another grazing. Before he had a chance to scream, the bus sandwiched him between it and the car. Crushed. Cries of children erupted from the bus. A few seconds of claustrophobic terror and the bus pulled away. Sid had held on. Just.

Max reached out the window and pulled up Sid's legs. Sid grappled his fingers around the doorframe and pulled himself onto the roof, leaving a perfectly formed indentation of himself on the side of the car.

"Don't let them crash us," a kid yelled out.

Sid used his head to shatter a bus window and pulled himself on board with the help of a dozen arms.

Surrounded by the kids, Sid felt something strange. He felt validated. Validated and angry. For the first time he was surrounded by . . . small humany things . . . who didn't want to crash either. He had been unaware that there were others just like him.

"Let's get them," Sid yelled.

Running down the aisle, Sid was followed by a cavalry of children. The bigger kids took out the standing Thor, helped by the smaller kids who piled on top.

Grabbing Burnside in a headlock, Sid pulled him from the driver's seat. The bus swiped a parked car, almost sending it towards a group of children waiting at a stop.

A little human hand reached over and pulled the door release lever. The girl had watched the bus driver do this at every stop for the first year of school.

"I've always wanted to do that," she said.

Burnside bounced along the road, followed by his companion. The children cheered their efforts.

The kids at the bus stop stared in wonder as Crash Test Dummies tumbled in their direction.

"Cool," one said. "I saw it first. It's mine!"

Sid jumped into the driver's seat and slammed his foot on the brake.

Nothing.

30

The big blue expanse of water momentarily captivated Sid as the sun sparkled off the surface, looking like liquid diamonds. He didn't know this was a river. He hadn't seen such a magnificent sight before. Nor had he been behind the wheel of a bus before. He had no idea what to do. He just wanted to stop.

Sid panicked. He slammed the brakes again and again and again. Speeding down the steep hill, Sid saw the river nearing as the bus gathered pace. He screamed. It was contagious. First he thought a siren made the high-pitched noise behind him, before realising it came from twenty-nine screaming students. Sid thought the situation must be bad, and screamed again. He knew that heading to this big watery thing was not good. Pretending to faint was not an option. He turned to see the terror on the children's faces.

Gripping the wheel, Sid swung the bus tightly onto

Riverdale Drive. Children flew to one side of the bus, landing on the floor behind the seats. Sid pushed hard on the brake, almost dislocating his knee. Nothing. If he could swerve it enough to the right, he might make it onto the bridge, but the steering wheel was hard to shift.

The EnviroCar raced around the bend on Riverdale Drive, following the bus.

"They're going to go into the river," Layla yelled.

Max double checked his seat belt and pulled the strap so it would lock.

"Sebastian, you have to stop it." Max fumbled with Madison's belt.

Sebastian's instincts took over. He prepared to do what he did best. Crash. Speeding up, he overtook the bus and swerved into its path. The bus grill bore down, filling Sebastian's view.

Impact.

Tyres squealed as the car was dragged along the road. The front wheels of the bus crushed the car hood. Metal twisted and buckled. The car felt like being inside a jackhammer. The remaining windows exploded into the cabin. Glass held in the air with early morning sunlight glistening off the jagged edges. The car spun and was pulled under the out-of-control machine.

The bus spat out the EnviroCar, sending it into a spin. Skidding sideways across the road it hit an embankment and rolled. Broken pieces flew into the air. No one inside could tell how many times it flipped. It was just a blur as the ground and the sky spun in turn. Sliding on the roof, dirt sprayed inside the car. Beside the river it ground to a sickening halt.

Madison was ejected through the back window. In an instant she disappeared into the river, leaving only bubbles where she splashed down.

The bus had changed direction, enough to send it towards the bridge. The impact had only slowed it slightly. Terrified, Sid pulled on the handbrake until it bent. It had no effect. The wheels slipped on the road and hit the side of the bridge. The grill tore off the bus. Vibrating to a stop, everyone in the bus surged forward in a cascade of children and schoolbags.

Sid tried to hold onto the steering wheel. The force of the collision sent him airborne, torpedoing him through the windscreen. He hit the water and vanished.

Realising Madison was gone, Max looked to the water to where the splash had sent out ripples. Held upside-down by the seat belt, he groped at the buckle.

"Are you all right?" he asked Layla.

"I don't think I'm broken," she said, releasing her belt and falling onto the ceiling.

Twisting their bodies, they turned themselves upright.

"You're bleeding," Layla said.

Max touched the side of his head. Blood remained on his fingers.

"I'm going after Madison," said Max, as he climbed out the window.

Layla looked up to the empty seat. Sliding out of the opposite window, she saw Sebastian pinned under the car.

Only half his body was visible, with the rest twisted in unnatural ways – folded and disappearing into the crushed metal.

"Sebastian, you don't look so good," said Layla.

"I'm fine," replied Sebastian. "I'm a hero. This is what I do."

Layla peered over the spinning wheels of the upturned vehicle and spotted the bus hanging over the edge of the bridge. Children screamed as they piled towards the back of the bus, causing its weight to shift. She watched the bus slip and teeter on the mangled bridge railing.

"Stay there," Layla said as she ran towards the bridge.

"Do my best," Sebastian called back.

Layla ran onto the bridge and up the side of the bus. The door had crossed the railing and hung above the water. Small fists slammed against the windows, desperate to escape. Metal crowed as each movement took the bus closer to the river. It balanced like a giant seesaw with wheels. Unstrapping her backpack, Layla pulled out a coil of abseiling rope. Using a carabiner she attached it to the rear bumper. Running it across the bridge, she tied the rope to the opposite railing. It wouldn't be enough to hold, but it might keep the bus stable just long enough.

Stepping onto the bumper she reached up and pulled the handles of the emergency exit. The rubber seal came free, dislodging the window. Layla fell onto her backpack as the perspex window dropped on her. The bigger kids started pouring out of the bus, some stopping to help other kids climb down.

Scrambling around Layla, some children screamed as others began going into shock. From the bus she could hear the cries of children still trapped aboard.

Climbing through the window, Layla spotted a bunch of young kids huddled up the front. Easing down the aisle, she felt the bus moving beneath her feet. Almost reaching them, she held out her hand.

"You have to come with me right now," she ordered.

The bus lurched forward. A loud crack ricocheted through the air.

"Come on, you can do it," she whispered.

Slipping towards the river, the bridge railing ripped through the side of the bus, shattering windows, leaving a gouge of jagged and twisted metal.

"Move," she yelled. Metal squealed as the bus fell forward.

Kids raced towards the back. They clambered out the window, leaping to the children below. Layla followed, springing from the window as the barrier gave way and the rope snapped. The bus plummeted into the water.

Layla landed on the road, scraping her knees. The bus floated for a moment. Then sunk. Turned and floated up again. And finally disappeared.

Max pushed through the surface to catch his breath. His second attempt to find Madison failed. He paddled on the surface and watched the bus sink. Filling his lungs with air, he dove back into the river.

Max made another attempt and spotted Madison sinking in the murky river. Diving underwater, clouded in the muddy darkness, he reached for her hand and grabbed hold. She felt heavier than expected and pulled him down. The air escaped from Max's lungs. He felt his chest tighten.

Floating.

Calm.

He felt like he could stay there for eternity, locked inside the peace of the water. In the mist of the murky water, he swore he could see Ruby's face where Madison's should be, with the wisps of her hair floating against the darkening background.

Before he could think, his body automatically started struggling. The sunlight through the water resembled a single glaring headlight as Max swum towards it. Despite all that had been done to him — what he had put himself through, how Lucinda had destroyed his family and their future — he wanted to survive. He looked towards the water surface and hoped he could reach it.

Breaking through the surface, Max gasped for air. The day seemed brighter than he remembered. Taking the last few strokes, he grabbed a wooden boat tie at the waters edge.

"Climb up on me," Max said. He winced as Madison grabbed his hair and pulled until she made it onto the bank. In his wet clothing, Max rolled out of the water and onto the grass.

"Let's do it again," Madison squeaked.

"Let's not." Max held out his arm, preventing Madison from jumping back into the river.

Trying to grip his hand on the side of the car,

Sebastian's fingers grabbed at the air. His body fell back and his arm went limp. He lost strength. For a moment he understood why humans didn't like crashing. He had never seen such panic at a crash site before. At CrashCorp there was always excitement from the Crash Test Dummies, and analytical gazes from the human supervisors, but here there was no joy or cheering, only screaming and fear.

Sebastian watched Max and Madison run towards him. Max dripping wet. Madison stumbling. Max helped her to her synthetic feet.

"Sebastian," Max yelled.

"Dad," Madison cried.

Sebastian's eyes powered down.

Everything turned black.

Black.

Dead black.

31

The morning sun made the Hybrids' vision blurry as they walked out of the CrashCorp grounds for the first time. The world seemed bright, lit up by the glowing yellow ball in the sky. The Hybrids found it difficult to comprehend how much space surrounded them, as it seemed almost endless.

Some dummies became dizzy, overwhelmed. First the world went all the way to the fence. The driveway took them to more roads. Those roads took them to other roads. None had ever considered there could be so many roads, so many places to go. The more roads they found, the more roads they continued to find.

Confused witnesses thought they had stumbled onto the set of a horror movie. Some ran in fear. Some called emergency services. Others remained grounded in awe. Many had lived in the area for decades without ever knowing who their neighbours really were. After years of only watching each other go by, they were given an excuse to gather together.

A fire engine turned up first, followed by ambulances and the police. Callers claimed strange beings walked through the neighbourhood. At first the call-takers for emergency services wondered if they were receiving prank calls, or maybe the callers might be the ones in need of help. Then another call came. Then another.

All available police cars were diverted to the bridge and the surrounding areas.

A Crash Test Dummy ran in front of a police car and was launched over the roof. Cracking the windscreen, it landed on the road behind. The police car screeched to a stop. Two officers stepped from the vehicle to inspect the body. Vomit built up in the throat of the constable at the thought he had hit someone. He imagined there would be blood and a few human insides decorating the road. Hard chunks of breakfast filled his throat. He tried to swallow. Rounding the back of the police car, the constable saw the body lying on the road.

"What a shot," said the Hybrid. "Line me up for another, this time with the lights firing."

The police officer and his breakfast parted ways.

Both Hybrids and Thors commandeered the new test model EnviroCars. They emptied the car park as they drove from the CrashCorp grounds. Most didn't get very far before their instincts took hold, lining the roads with a series of crumpled vehicles.

One CrashCorp car drove erratically down the road.

Being driven by a Thor it swerved to hit the Hybrids; partly deliberate, partly because it had little idea how to control the EnviroCar. Hybrids went over the car, under the car, or were sideswiped and flew across the asphalt. It gave them a sense of joy only a crash could give a Crash Test Dummy. The Thor lost control and wrapped the car around the trunk of a Northfolk Pine.

Local residents would later appear in newspaper articles and news videos recalling the events.

"You just can't tell what's going on behind closed doors. Especially at these big companies, they never tell you anything."

"We've never really had a problem before. I mean, there were trucks going in and out, but I never thought they would be keeping anyone . . . or anything held captive."

"We had heard rumours. We never thought any to be true, they just seemed so fanciful."

Neighbours exchanged stories with each other over the fence, discussing the events they imagined occurred inside CrashCorp. Even long afterwards, the residents would often gather to talk about the secrets the factory had been keeping. Whether the secrets were true and correct didn't matter as it gave occasion to have a little gossip with tea.

Kym was driven to the scene, along with Layla's parents. They had been out searching all night. Kym had asked if she could ride in the helicopter with the Police Air Wing. They politely refused.

It wasn't long before crowds gathered at the final accident site. Nearby streets were closed off and the morning traffic quickly backed up. Parents hurried to the site to find their children. Helicopters hovered overhead, as authorities attempted to comprehend the scale of the destruction. The internet lit up with posts of first-hand accounts. News crews set up live broadcasts from the scene as the city paused to tune in.

During a broadcast, a car covered with yellow and black caution stickers rolled along the road, being pushed by a team of Hybrids. Witnesses were stunned to see Lucinda strapped into the driver's seat, screaming words many didn't even care to repeat in police statements.

*   *   *

Max sat down in the gutter and stared at the wall he had graffitied several weeks earlier. The painting of the alien being sucked into the black hole was gone, lost forever under the layers of fresh paint. Like many memories — like former Crash Test Dummies on the Wall of Honour — the only evidence now remained in a photograph. Photographs captured how people once were, a single instant that could never be repeated. They captured the moments otherwise forgotten and wiped from memory.

After the accident, Max and Layla were both admitted to hospital for observation. So was Kym, who had collapsed after seeing Max. Memories came flooding back as paramedics wheeled her into the hospital on a stretcher. While hugging Max she saw Madison awkwardly shadowing him, and pulled her in. Hugging Madison was like she was hugging her own daughter. Kym cried hard and loud. Through the haze of tears she swore she could see Ruby's face.

Nurses recognised their old friend and colleague, as she was unloaded from the ambulance.

Over the next couple of days, faces flashed in front of Kym. Faces from the past. Friendly faces. Through the handholding and tears, Kym began to speak of the year since Daniel and Ruby died. She told how she ignored her friends and shut out the world. She told of how she did anything to forget. She told of her shame. How hopeless she felt when she saw her family being wheeled into the hospital. How she began walking around the streets at night, collecting things just to fill the void, thinking one day she would make something worthwhile of it all, afraid to admit she had collected piles of worthless junk.

Max shared a hospital room with Layla, where they were monitored until the shock wore off. Searching on Layla's phone, Max found a video from the accident site. He watched in disbelief. Max leapt onto Layla's bed and crawled in next to her. Together they watched the video, which had over four million hits.

The handheld footage displayed frightened school children, assembled together for comfort and safety around Layla. Max watched as his mother embraced him and Madison. The camera turned to see a battered car being pushed by Hybrids. The camera zoomed in on Lucinda trapped in the front seat.

"Let me out of here. I don't deserve this," she screamed.

Witnesses watched in stunned silence.

The video tracked back to Max. He watched himself walk away from his mother. Kym pulled Madison closer.

"I'll take care of you, baby girl," Max remembered her gasping. Kym held Madison tight. Overwhelmed, Kym sobbed until she blew snot bubbles out her nose. Madison wacked her in the face, trying to pop them.

They watched Max storm over to the car. Anger and exhaustion ruled his face. Lucinda screamed and hollered and shrieked about how she had been so unjustly treated.

"You can't do this to me" she screamed. "They're hurting me."

"Shut up," Max yelled at Lucinda. "Just because you scream the loudest, doesn't mean you feel the most pain. There are people here a lot worse off, and it's all because of you."

Lucinda's jaw dropped in feigned offence. "I've never been spoken to like that before in all my life," she lied. "How dare you?"

Through the news broadcast, a voice Max considered insignificant had been released to the world. Max did something he never thought he would. He talked. And talked. And talked. He talked until he became used to the pain, until he understood it. He talked about how he felt like he had been moving through wet cement since the first crash. How he thought talking was a waste of time, as it didn't change the past. He talked until he finally had a decent night sleep.

He repainted his graffiti the night after leaving the

hospital. The evening walk cleared his head. Crossing the train tracks, moving through the shadows and empty streets, Max ventured on a mission to paint over the past. Max painted Elcycer, or what he thought it would be like based on what Sebastian had told him. Roads networked into a surreal maze, populated by cars and dummies crashing. Crash Test Dummies took their place amongst the greats and were honoured as heroes. After hearing of Max's effort at the bus accident the building owner was happy to give Max permission to complete his graffiti, and dropped the earlier charges.

Kym's friends started trickling over to the house. Soon it became a flood, with the house full of people helping her clean. A garbage skip appeared out the front, when it was full another took its place. After the last load was taken away, a steam cleaner came for the carpet. Kym drank nothing but tea.

In Daniel's office – Max's father – his designs for the solar powered paint and the fuel cells used on the EnviroCar were found, locked away in his safe. Alongside were documents that Daniel had collected, showing he believed CrashCorp were using his designs without permission. His prototypes and blueprints were handed to the police. They were identical to the ones Lucinda claimed she had invented — and destroyed lives for — so she could claim the work as her own. The designs later appeared as evidence in the double murder trial against Lucinda, for using Crash Test Dummies to cause the accident that took Daniel's and Ruby's lives.

CrashCorp was shut down and the dummies were adopted by homes in the community. Strangely enough, the school children waiting at the bus stop during the chase reported only one dummy falling from the moving bus: Burnside was never found. Some people say that he ran away before the police came; another rumour circulated that, for five dollars, he could be viewed where he remains hidden in one of the student's basements.

Sid made his way out of the river. Eventually. He was found days after the crash when he stepped out on the riverbank a few kilometres upstream. Sid's dislike for crashing, and for his gallant effort of stopping the bus, gained the trust of the children and the public. Louis decided to take early retirement and Sid took over the position of bus driver. Louis also decided to spend a long, long time on an island far, far away. Even shop mannequins still give him shivers.

Layla's parents decided to stop moving around, at least until she finished High School. They had received more media attention than they could ever wish for – much more than they ever had when doing pageants. So much so, they no longer desired it and sought life away from the spotlight. They allowed Layla to keep her treehouse. Her parents finally finished her bedroom, and while it was comfortable, she didn't use it much. Layla's mum realised her daughter may not be perfect, but at least she still had a daughter.

Clean and full of sunlight once again, the sound of laughter echoed through the house as Max chased Madison around. Max helped her explore the outside world and she found wonderment in everything. Butterflies, tomatoes, buttons. He taught her how to cross the road so she could avoid cars. Even Emperor Norton tolerated her. Sometimes.

A team of engineers flew in from Washington after watching the online footage. They worked day and night for more than two weeks as they tried to reconstruct Sebastian, using many parts found in the shipping container at the recycling yard.

The day Sebastian moved in with Max, they had their portrait taken. Kym and Sebastian stood at the back, Madison and Max at the front. Their smiles captured forever.

At nights Sebastian wandered out into Max's back yard, or ventured all the way to the deck of Layla's treehouse. He looked up at the sky. For hours he stared up to the planet Jupiter. When Sebastian was reconstructed, a part of Jupiter was used. It was a small circuit that regulated electronic impulses – the closest thing to being an actual Crash Test Dummy's heart – Jupiter's heart.

One morning the newspaper arrived. On the front cover was a feature article about Sebastian. The story detailed the investigation into how Sebastian had knocked the bus off course, preventing it from plummeting into the river, saving the lives of twenty-nine children, although it had cost him his own life – at the time. Max read the one word headline aloud.

Sebastian grabbed the newspaper and smiled at the

photo of himself. He held up the paper and pointed at the headline.

"Can you read that again?" he asked.

"Hero," said Max.

ABOUT THE AUTHOR

David Phoebe is an Australian based author, living in Melbourne. He has studied *Professional Writing and Editing*, *Professional Screenwriting (Film, TV and Digital Media)*, *Justice*, and *Criminal Justice Administration*. He has published articles in newspapers and magazines throughout Australia.

Captive Humans: True Crime Cases of People Held Captive was his first full-length adult book. *Sebastian: Crash Test Dummy* is his first novel for young people.

David works in the field of criminal justice and lives with his rescued cat. He likes cats. A lot.

www.ingramcontent.com/pod-product-compliance
Lightning Source LLC
Chambersburg PA
CBHW060915180626
46817CB00004B/1268